AN
APPETITE
FOR
PASSION
COOKBOOK

*One cannot think well, love well, sleep well,
if one has not dined well.*

—VIRGINIA WOOLF

AN
APPETITE
FOR
PASSION

COOKBOOK

❧

Foreword by
LAURA ESQUIVEL

Edited and compiled by
IVANA LOWELL AND LISA FINE

Introduction and text by
JOHN WILLOUGHBY

Recipe testing and development by
ANN SWAIN CATERING

MIRAMAX
B O O K S
HYPERION
N E W Y O R K

For information address:
HYPERION
114 Fifth Avenue, New York, NY 10011

Art Direction & Design
INDIKA NYC, INC.

Illustration for Indika NYC, Inc.
LUCRETIA MORONI AND SCOTT REES

Library of Congress Cataloging-in-Publication Data:

An appetite for passion : cookbook / foreword by Laura Esquivel :
introduction and text by John Willoughby : edited and compiled by Lisa
Fine and Ivana Lowell : recipe testing and development by Ann Swain
Catering—1st ed.
p.   cm.
Includes index.
ISBN 0-7868-6162-2
1. Cookery   I. Willoughby, John.   II. Fine, Lisa.   III. Lowell, Ivana.
TX714.A65   1995   94–48517
641.5—dc20   CIP

FIRST EDITION

1   3   5   7   9   10   8   6   4   2

Contents

Common folk, among all peoples, use sayings to express their wisdom. I frequently make use of them because they hold great universal truths. One that all of you here will recognize is "Like water for chocolate," and another of my favorites is "The payment for love is love." Nothing truer can be said. The only asset equivalent to love is love itself. Neither gold nor Quetzal feathers nor precious stones can equal it. Its value stands above any other. I find that anything that is worthwhile is realized by and with love.

From its conception, *Like Water for Chocolate* was bathed in love. Its gestation did not begin when the central idea of the story occurred to me but, rather, when I received my first food, given with love.

I wrote my novel with the intention of giving the transferring of love in the kitchen the appreciation it deserves. I am convinced, just as Tita is in my novel, that we can impregnate food with emotion, just as we can every other activity we engage in. When this affective charge is powerful, it is impossible for it to pass unnoticed. Others feel it, touch it, enjoy it. I find confirmation of that each day that passes. I wrote my novel with love; my agents, my editors, my translators, my distributors, have felt it, have shared it with me, and have infected others. This book is the last link in that chain of love. And I am more than satisfied with the "payment" my work has received in return.

So then, there is nothing left for me to do but thank all the living and the dead, those present and absent, who contributed their air, earth, fire, and water to cooking up an "appetite for passion." The existence of this book reconciles me with the belief that in questions of love and cooking there are no frontiers. Every meal I have eaten, the person with whom I have eaten it, and how it was eaten have determined who I am. In this vein, I would like to take a minute to confess how it is that a modest amount of Coca-Cola flows through my veins.

It happened this way. Everyone knows that my mother's family is from Piedras Negras, on the northern border of Mexico. For me, Piedras Negras began in the state of Coahuila and ended in San Antonio, Texas. Its city limits were quite expansive, or so it seemed to me. That undoubtedly was because as a girl I had no concept of geography. The business of "From this tree over to the creek" is a different matter—geography, I just couldn't learn. All I understood was that there were places where I felt at home. I had to spend several years in school before I mastered the fact that things like borders exist, or hatred between two peoples. My family traveled every year from Mexico City to San Antonio, Texas, to visit relatives. On the way, we always stopped to visit friends in Piedras Negras. At each place, the magic was repeated: alchemy in the kitchen, ceremony, the powerful transferral of love through food. The only difference was that if in Piedras Negras we devoured flour tortillas, *machaca* and eggs, and *dulce de leche* with nuts, in San Antonio I feasted on glazed doughnuts and Milky Ways. On the other hand, as Ariel Dorfman and Armand Mattelart had not yet written *How to Read Donald Duck*, I did not get indigestion reading Walt Disney comics on the trip.

And so the years went by and my knowledge of geography grew. I made notable advances. Before long, I realized that Piedras Negras did not stretch as far as San Antonio: one city was in the United States and the other in Mexico; there was a border between them; and, furthermore, the culture of Mexico had little to do with that of the United States. No matter that every Saturday night my sisters and I organized parties where we served sandwiches and Coca-Colas, danced rock and roll, and chewed gum. We found an explanation for everything: the sandwiches were a variation on *tortas,* and *tortas*— well, you didn't need to know *their* origin, they were Mexican, period. Our taste for chewing gum comes to us from the Aztecs. Long before the arrival of the Spaniards, Indians were chewing *chapopote.* There was nothing wrong with rock and roll, it was a worldwide phenomenon, and Coca-Cola—well, that had been created for medicinal purposes and should be good for you, shouldn't it?

The years rolled by, and my knowledge of geography grew. I learned where Vietnam was. I learned it was divided into two parts. I learned that my cousin in San Antonio had been called into the army. That was when Coca-Cola began to taste bitter to me. I learned that it ate the enamel off your teeth and was bad for your health. We began calling it "the black waters of Yankee imperialism." I stopped

Foreword

drinking it. I was afraid it might transmit the horror of war. Fortunately, hippies appeared on my geographical map. I learned where the University of California at Berkeley was, and what was happening there. In Mexico, too, we young people took to the streets and handed out flowers and listened to Joan Baez and laughed and celebrated free love and thought the birth of the "New Man" was possible—in short, we believed we could change the world. And . . . well, we couldn't. For a long time, I wondered where we went wrong.

Why was it that none of the revolutions we took part in succeeded in creating a system favorable to the emergence of that New Man? Where had all the hippies gone? Was Joan Baez still singing? Who were the children of Woodstock?

The success of my novel gave me the answers. Because of it I traveled throughout the Americas and came to realize I was not the only one preoccupied with establishing a new relationship with the earth, with the universe, with the sacred. Like me, many people had discovered that the new revolution was going to germinate in the world of the personal, in rituals, in ceremonies. Many people, like myself, were trying desperately to counterpose spiritual values to material ones. Many people, like myself, had conserved the power of fire in their homes—the palpable proof of which is *Like Water for Chocolate*.

And this book is something more: the confirmation that I was right when I was a child. There are no frontiers! It's a lie that a dividing line can separate one people from another. It's a lie that the hippies sang in vain—they sowed a seed. It's a lie that people in the United States don't eat chilis and frijoles—they love them. It's a lie that we Mexicans don't eat hamburgers—we do so with gusto, we just add a little *salsa picante*.

I know now that hope still lives, that the New Man is en route, that he will be a person completely ignorant of geography, that it will not matter to him on which side of the line the soil beneath his feet lies, that he will take as much pleasure from eating a tortilla as from drinking a Coca-Cola because he will be aware that it is not what he is ingesting that matters, but that he is participating in a ceremony that will transport him back to his origins, to his cosmic origins, which lie far beyond ethnicity. For if we return to the cosmic, we

Mexicans are children of the maize, and people in the United States have eaten enough popcorn by now to be counted as kin.

Addendum:
machaca: dried, shredded beef
dulce de leche: a caramelized milk sweet
torta: large roll with savory filling
chapopote: a natural tar

Translated by Margaret Sayers Peden

INTRODUCTION: *FOOD, MAGIC, PASSION*

The act of cooking has many possible faces. On one hand, it is simply about providing nourishment; on the other, it can be a kind of sorcery. For food cooked with care and love is not just bodily fuel, but a ribbon of sensual pleasure that weaves its way through our daily lives.

Seldom has this passionate aspect of food been more imaginatively explored than in the film *Like Water for Chocolate*. In the hands of author Laura Esquivel and director Alfonso Arau, eating and cooking became sensuous, inflammatory events. For many who saw it, the film provided a renewed connection to food, to passion, to family, and to the way these three can interact to bring a sort of magic into our lives.

In fact, food has a long history as a tool for working magic. Many cultures have believed that particular ingredients or dishes could alter human behavior, and a cook who could go into the kitchen with ordinary foodstuffs and emerge with complex, deeply flavorful dishes was considered something very close to a sorcerer.

Among the many ways that food has been alleged to mysteriously influence our behavior, none has been more widely touted nor more eagerly sought than the power of food as an instigator of passion, an inducement to love, an aphrodisiac. This makes perfect sense. Over the centuries, literally thousands of foods have been considered aphrodisiacs, usually because of their physical appearance, their association with fertility, or their exotic rarity.

In earlier days, for example, the "Doctrine of Signatures" taught that the shape of any particular object was a sort of divine hint at its use. To believers in this world view, it was only logical that foods from bananas to eggplant to oysters and figs should have the power to enhance sex.

Foods that were new, exotic, and expensive also became aphrodisiacs. When rare and luxurious spices arrived in the West from the East, for example, they were so stimulating to the senses that they were reputed to enhance sexual desire and passion—as if by magic.

Elaborate rituals were often devised for the consumption of

aphrodisiacs. In seventeenth-century Paris, certain restaurants served elaborate aphrodisiac menus in rooms where the doors had no outside knobs and the table was set next to a bed. Across the ocean in Mexico, a Mayan woman with an errant husband would be instructed to adorn herself with a garland of a particular flower and bathe in scented water by the light of the moon. If she then cooked a dish containing some of the flowers and some of the bathwater, her husband would return, more ardent than ever before.

Like many other myths, legends, and taboos surrounding food, the concept of aphrodisiacs may well veil some scientific truth. Researchers have recently discovered, for instance, that chocolate contains large amounts of phenylethylamine, a stimulant that is very similar to chemicals released by the human body during sex.

But more importantly, food spurs passion because eating is about both survival and about indulging our capacity for physical pleasure. When foods are rare and exotic, or perfumed with spices, or rich with the complex taste of chocolate, or fresh and briny like oysters, consuming them stimulates every one of our senses.

In these pages you will find recipes for many dishes inspired by the magic realism of the film *Like Water for Chocolate*. They come from the kitchens of celebrated hostesses as well as some of America's foremost chefs. Some make imaginative use of spices and other ingredients such as figs, pomegranates, and caviar; others employ the earthy, complex flavor combinations of the American Southwest. Despite their rich flavors, many are light and healthful (these recipes are indicated with the ▨ symbol), for bodily passions can perhaps best be stirred by foods that are good for the body.

Ultimately, though, the secret of these passionate foods does not lie in ingredients, nor in spells or rituals. Rather, it lies in the simple enjoyment that can come from preparing and eating food with zest and fervor. Inhaling the scent of herbs as you crush them, watching shards of dark chocolate melt into a seductive puddle, or letting the juice from a bite of mango slip down your chin, your appetite for passion will be kindled. As Tita says in the film, "The trick is to make it with lots of love."

—JOHN WILLOUGHBY

Only dull people are brilliant at breakfast.

—OSCAR WILDE, *An Ideal Husband*

❦BREAKFASTS❦

BANANA PANCAKES
WITH COCONUT SYRUP

Adapted from Mesa Mexicana *by Mary Sue Milliken and Susan Feniger*

Bananas are one of the world's most popular fruits, and also one of the fruits most widely credited with aphrodisiac powers. Their image received a definite boost some years ago from legendary dancer-singer Josephine Baker, who made her stage debut in Paris clad in nothing but a girdle of bananas.

Simple and delicious, these fluffy pancakes from the Border Grill in Santa Monica, California, provide a tropical twist to an old breakfast staple. Strawberries or blueberries can be substituted for the bananas if you wish. Serves 4 to 6.

> 1 1/2 CUPS ALL-PURPOSE FLOUR
> 1 TABLESPOON SUGAR
> 1/2 TEASPOON SALT
> 1 TEASPOON BAKING SODA
> 1 TEASPOON BAKING POWDER
> 1 LARGE EGG
> 1 CUP BUTTERMILK
> 1/4 CUP WHOLE MILK
> 1 TABLESPOON UNSALTED BUTTER, MELTED
> ABOUT 3 TABLESPOONS UNSALTED BUTTER
> 3 RIPE BANANAS, CUT INTO 1/3-INCH SLICES

Sift together the flour, sugar, salt, baking soda, and baking powder. Set aside.

In a large bowl, whisk together the egg, buttermilk, whole milk, and melted butter. Add the dry ingredients and stir until the flour just disappears. The batter should be lumpy.

Preheat the oven to 200°F. Melt 1/2 tablespoon of the butter in a large cast-iron skillet over medium heat. Ladle about 1/4 cup of the batter into the pan for each pancake. Immediately press 4 or 5 banana slices into each, so the batter oozes slightly over the fruit. Cook until bubbles appear and then flip and brown on the other side, about 3 minutes total. Transfer the pancakes to a platter and keep warm in the oven while you cook the remaining batches, adding butter to the pan as needed. Serve hot, topped with warm coconut syrup.

COCONUT SYRUP

> 1 (14^1/$_2$-OUNCE) CAN UNSWEETENED COCONUT MILK
> 1 CUP SWEETENED SHREDDED COCONUT
> 3/4 CUP PACKED BROWN SUGAR

Combine all the ingredients in a heavy saucepan. Bring to a boil over medium heat, reduce the heat to low, and cook 20 minutes, stirring occasionally. Transfer to a blender and purée until smooth. Serve warm. May be stored, covered and refrigerated, up to 2 weeks. Makes about 2 cups.

"Owing to its shape the banana has been used in black
magic ceremonies . . . there is an Apache love chant which says,
'I look at him
I give him the banana
As the banana is with the man
So will the man be with me.'"
—BARBARA CARTLAND

HUEVOS RANCHEROS

Adapted from The Maidstone Inn, East Hampton, NY

Eggs are so provocative that the entire last chapter of the Persian erotic classic *The Perfumed Garden* is devoted to the beneficial effects of egg yolks on lovemaking. Over the centuries, they have been used in many fantastical potions designed to increase sexual vigor. However, they might be most effective when enjoyed on a lazy morning with a hot and spicy tomato sauce, warm tortillas, and a sprinkling of cheese. Serves 4.

> 1/4 CUP VEGETABLE OIL FOR FRYING
> 4 LARGE CORN TORTILLAS
> 8 LARGE EGGS
> SALT AND FRESHLY GROUND BLACK PEPPER
> ABOUT 2 CUPS RANCHERO SALSA, WARMED IN A
>   SAUCEPAN (OPPOSITE)
> 1 CUP GRATED JACK OR CHEDDAR CHEESE
> 2 TABLESPOONS CHOPPED PARSLEY

Preheat the oven to 200°F.

In a large skillet, heat the oil over medium heat until hot but not smoking. Fry the tortillas one at a time for 3 or 4 seconds on each side, just until soft. Drain on paper towels, wrap in aluminum foil, and place in the warm oven.

Break 4 eggs into the pan, sprinkle with salt and pepper to taste, and fry as preferred. Transfer to a large plate, place in the oven, and fry the other 4 eggs.

Set a tortilla on each of 4 plates. Place 2 eggs on top of each tortilla, and spoon a generous helping of salsa over the eggs. (For a traditional appearance, spoon the salsa over the whites, leaving the yolks exposed.) Sprinkle with cheese and parsley and serve hot.

RANCHERO SALSA

1 TABLESPOON VEGETABLE OIL
$^1/_2$ SMALL ONION, CHOPPED
1 GARLIC CLOVE, MINCED
ABOUT 4 CUPS FINELY CHOPPED FRESH OR
    (DRAINED) CANNED TOMATOES
2 JALAPEÑO CHILE PEPPERS, STEMMED, SEEDED, AND CHOPPED
1 TEASPOON LIME JUICE
1 TEASPOON SUGAR
SALT AND FRESHLY GROUND PEPPER TO TASTE

In a medium-sized skillet, heat the oil over medium heat until hot. Add the onion and sauté, stirring occasionally, for 3 minutes. Add the garlic and cook, stirring occasionally, for 2 to 3 more minutes or until the onion is transparent. Add all remaining ingredients and simmer, stirring once in a while, for about 15 minutes or until slightly thickened. Will keep about 5 days, covered and refrigerated. Makes about 4 cups.

"Love and eggs should be fresh to be enjoyed."
—RUSSIAN PROVERB

HUEVOS CON CHORIZO
(SCRAMBLED EGGS WITH SPICY SAUSAGE)

Adapted from Rick Bayless, Frontera Grill, Chicago, IL

As the source of life itself, eggs have connections with the divine and the sacred that go back to ancient times. Not surprisingly, they have also been a symbol of sex and fertility in virtually every civilization. Here these tidy little packages of inspiration are served up fluffy and rich with spicy sausage and accompanied by warm corn tortillas. Serves 4.

> 1/2 POUND CHORIZO SAUSAGE, CASING REMOVED
> 1 TABLESPOON VEGETABLE OIL
> 1/2 YELLOW ONION, DICED FINE
> 1 LARGE RIPE TOMATO, CORED AND ROUGHLY CHOPPED
> 8 LARGE EGGS, WELL BEATEN
> SALT AND FRESHLY GROUND PEPPER TO TASTE
> 1/2 CUP QUESO BLANCO (YOU MAY SUBSTITUTE GRATED
>   JACK CHEESE)
> 2 TABLESPOONS ROUGHLY CHOPPED FRESH PARSLEY
> 8 CORN TORTILLAS (OPTIONAL)

Put the chorizo and vegetable oil in a skillet and cook over medium-low heat for 10 minutes, stirring occasionally to break up the sausage. Remove the sausage with a slotted spoon, drain off all but 2 tablespoons of fat, add the onion and tomato, and sauté until the onion is soft, about 7 minutes. Return the sausage to the pan.

Beat the eggs with the salt and pepper until just combined. Add to the skillet and scramble until done to your liking. Scoop into a warm dish, crumble queso blanco on top, sprinkle with parsley, and serve accompanied by warm corn tortillas and tomatillo sauce (see page 59).

Note: Tortillas can be warmed in the microwave by wrapping them in a damp dish towel and microwaving for 2 minutes on high.

PASSIONATE FRUIT PLATTER

Serves 2 generously.

> 1 PAPAYA, SEEDED, PEELED, AND THINLY SLICED LENGTHWISE
> 1/2 HONEYDEW, SEEDED, PEELED, AND THINLY SLICED
>   LENGTHWISE
> 2 MANGOES, PITTED, PEELED, AND CUT INTO BITE-SIZED
>   CHUNKS
> 1/2 CUP RASPBERRIES
> 1/2 CUP SEEDLESS GREEN GRAPES, HALVED
> JUICE OF 2 LIMES
> 1 TABLESPOON WILDFLOWER HONEY
> MINT SPRIGS AND NASTURTIUMS FOR GARNISH (OPTIONAL)

Fan out the papaya and melon slices on a plate, overlapping them slightly.

In a medium-sized bowl, combine the mangoes, raspberries, and grapes. Combine the lime juice and honey in a glass, mix until of an even consistency, add to the bowl of fruit, and toss gently.

Spoon the contents of the bowl over the papaya and honeydew slices and garnish with mint sprigs and nasturtiums, if desired.

"Man is only truly great when he acts from his passions."
—BENJAMIN DISRAELI

After a perfect meal we are more susceptible to the ecstasy of love than at any other time.

—Dr. Hans Balzi

❧STARTERS & SOUPS❧

LUSTY OYSTERS
WITH GINGER AND LIME

Marla Trump

Marla Trump, wife of tycoon Donald Trump, favors this stimulating starter when entertaining. Like lovers, some flavors seem made for each other, and ginger and lime are one of those perfect culinary marriages. Here they are served over oysters, perhaps the world's most well-known aphrodisiac. Grilling the oysters lightly adds a smoky flavor to further enhance their appeal. Serves 4 as an appetizer.

> 6 TABLESPOONS SALTED BUTTER AT ROOM TEMPERATURE
> 1/4 BUNCH CILANTRO, CLEANED AND CHOPPED
> 2 TEASPOONS FINELY MINCED FRESH GINGER
> 2 TABLESPOONS LIME JUICE
> 2 CLOVES GARLIC, ROASTED IN A 350°F OVEN FOR
>   20 MINUTES, PEELED
> 20 SHUCKED OYSTERS, DRAINED
> 1 TABLESPOON OLIVE OIL

In a blender or food processor, combine the butter, cilantro, ginger, lime juice, and roasted garlic cloves and process until smooth. Transfer the mixture to an 8-inch square of waxed paper and form into a roll about 1 inch in diameter. If the butter does not hold its form, place in the refrigerator until it just holds its shape well.

Place the oysters under the broiler or on the grill over a medium-hot fire and cook until firm to the touch, about 2 to 3 minutes per side. While the oysters are still warm, top each with a teaspoon or so of the ginger-lime butter; butter should melt over the oyster.
Serve immediately.

"Oysters are the most tender and delicate of all seafoods. They stay in bed all day and night. They never work or take any exercise, are stupendous drinkers and wait for their meals to come to them."

—HECTOR BOLITHO, *The Glorious Oyster*

ROSA'S GUACAMOLE

Rosa Mexicana, New York, NY

The Aztec word for avocado, *ahuacatl*, literally translates as "testicle." Apparently this was taken quite seriously, for Aztec virgins were forced to stay inside when avocados were being harvested. There is no record as to whether these maidens were allowed to actually eat the nutty-tasting, slippery fruit.

In this smooth-chunky version of the classic avocado dip, mashing the avocados with the back of a wooden spoon is a sensuous experience in itself. Serves 4.

6 TABLESPOONS FINELY CHOPPED WHITE ONION
2 TABLESPOONS CHOPPED JALAPEÑOS, SEEDS DISCARDED
1 TABLESPOON CHOPPED FRESH CILANTRO
1 TEASPOON SALT
2 RIPE AVOCADOS
1/4 CUP CHOPPED TOMATO, SEEDS AND JUICE DISCARDED
SALT AND FRESHLY GROUND BLACK PEPPER TO TASTE

In a large bowl, using the back of a wooden spoon, thoroughly mash the following ingredients: 2 tablespoons of the chopped onion, 1 teaspoon of jalapeño, 1 teaspoon of cilantro, and the teaspoon of salt.

Cut the avocados in half lengthwise, remove the pits, and scoop the meat out with a large spoon. In a separate bowl, thoroughly mash the avocado and fold in the mashed onion mixture and all the remaining ingredients. Season with salt and pepper to taste.

Note: If the guacamole is not going to be served immediately, place in a container and squeeze a small amount of lemon juice to cover the top. Cover with plastic wrap so that the wrap is actually touching the entire top surface of the guacamole and refrigerate. This should keep the guacamole from turning brown.

ARTICHOKE AND CRABMEAT TEASER

Marguerite Littman

Marguerite Littman, an expatriate from the American South now living in London, is a near-legendary hostess. Everyone from David Hockney to the Princess of Wales has dined at her table, and many of them have savored these little teasers.

Eating artichokes has often been compared to foreplay, which may explain why this edible thistle rates high among aphrodisiac foods. When Catherine de Médicis wed Henry II of France, she scandalized the French court with her inordinate fondness for artichokes; it was thought quite inappropriate for a young woman to be so addicted to an aphrodisiac. However, there is no record of any complaints from King Henry. Serves 4.

4 GLOBE ARTICHOKES

JUICE OF 1 LEMON

3 TABLESPOONS BUTTER

1/4 CUP FINELY CHOPPED SCALLIONS

3 STALKS OF CELERY, FINELY CHOPPED

1 GREEN BELL PEPPER, SEEDED AND FINELY CHOPPED

1 FRESH CHILE PEPPER OF YOUR CHOICE, SEEDED AND
    FINELY CHOPPED

3/4 CUP FISH STOCK

1/4 CUP DRY WHITE WINE

1/4 CUP HEAVY CREAM

1 TEASPOON CORNSTARCH DISSOLVED IN 1 TABLESPOON WATER

1/4 TEASPOON SALT

GENEROUS DASH GROUND RED PEPPER (CAYENNE), OR
    MORE TO PLEASE YOUR PALATE

1 POUND LUMP CRABMEAT, PICKED OVER WELL

1 SMALL BUNCH CILANTRO, CLEANED AND FINELY CHOPPED

GENEROUS DASH OF BRANDY

Remove artichoke stems and cut off the top quarter of each artichoke. Add the lemon juice to a large pot of boiling salted water and cook the artichokes until tender, about 20 minutes or until the outer leaves are easily removed. Drain, refresh with cold water, and leave to cool upside down. When cool enough to handle, pull out the inner leaves and scoop out the remaining choke.

In a small sauté pan over medium heat, melt the butter and sauté the scallions, celery, green pepper, and chile until tender but not brown, about 5 minutes, stirring constantly. Remove from the heat and add the fish stock, wine, cream, dissolved cornstarch, and salt and pepper and stir until smooth. Add the crabmeat, cilantro, and brandy, turn heat to low, and cook, stirring constantly, for 5 minutes or until the crabmeat is warmed through. Be careful not to break up the lumps of crabmeat. The sauce should be creamy and not thick. Spoon the mixture into the four warm prepared artichokes.

SPICY SHRIMP COCKTAIL
Adapted from Martha Stewart Living

Like other types of seafood, shrimp are a legendary aphrodisiac. In the days just before the dawn of the Roman Empire, Romans and Carthaginians alike favored these little crustaceans as a prelude to lovemaking, each city boasting that its shrimp were more delicious— and more effective.

Shrimp cocktail is a classic start to an intimate dinner. It's elegant, it can be prepared in advance, and there is something enticing about dipping those little shrimp in sauce and eating them one by one. Serves 4.

2 BAY LEAVES
1 TABLESPOON PEPPERCORNS
2 SMALL PIECES OF FRESH GINGERROOT, PEELED
1 CARROT, PEELED AND ROUGHLY CHOPPED
1 STALK CELERY, ROUGHLY CHOPPED
1/2 ONION, STUCK WITH 4 CLOVES
1 BUNCH PARSLEY STEMS
1 BUNCH THYME SPRIGS
2 DOZEN LARGE SHRIMP, SHELLED AND DEVEINED

Fill a large stock pot with water. Add all the ingredients except the shrimp and bring to a boil over high heat. Reduce the heat to low and simmer for 15 minutes. Add the shrimp and cook for 1 to 2 minutes, or until shrimp are opaque throughout. Drain, discard everything but the shrimp, and immediately plunge the shrimp into a large bowl of ice water to stop cooking. Cover and refrigerate until cool, then serve with jalapeño-cilantro sauce.

JALAPEÑO-CILANTRO COCKTAIL SAUCE

2 (28-OUNCE) CANS TOMATOES
1 1/2 TABLESPOONS CIDER VINEGAR
2 TABLESPOONS SUGAR
1/4 TEASPOON SALT
1/2 TEASPOON FRESHLY GROUND BLACK PEPPER
1/4 TEASPOON GROUND ALLSPICE
1/4 TEASPOON GROUND CLOVES
1/4 TEASPOON GROUND GINGER
1/4 TEASPOON GROUND RED PEPPER (CAYENNE)
PINCH OF DRY MUSTARD
2 TABLESPOONS GRATED FRESH GINGERROOT
2 TABLESPOONS CHOPPED FRESH CILANTRO
1 TEASPOON FINELY CHOPPED JALAPEÑO PEPPER
JUICE OF 3 LIMES

Push the tomatoes and their juice through a strainer or food mill.
Place in a large nonaluminum saucepan and add the sugar, salt, black
and red pepper, allspice, cloves, ground ginger, and mustard. Bring to
a boil over medium heat, reduce the heat to low, and simmer for
about 50 minutes or until slightly thinner than store-bought ketchup.
Remove from the heat and allow to cool to room temperature. Add
the grated gingerroot, cilantro, jalapeño, and lime juice. Refrigerate,
covered, for at least 1 hour. Adjust seasoning and serve.

CORN CAKES WITH CRÈME FRAÎCHE AND CAVIARS

Anne Rosenzweig, Arcadia, New York, NY

The more rare and expensive a food, the more exalted its reputation for promoting sexual desire. That equation makes caviar just about the number-one food of love. It is even said that Catherine II of Russia, although a legendary seductress, was unable to conceive a child until the night she served one of her paramours vast quantities of caviar before making love.

Corn cakes may not seem like luxury food, but in the hands of Anne Rosenzweig they become a sensory delight. Paired with caviar and silky crème fraîche, these little cakes consistently have everyone wishing for more. Serves 6—or 3 if you're not careful.

> 1 1/2 CUPS FRESH CORN KERNELS
> 1/2 CUP MILK
> 1/3 CUP CORNMEAL
> 1/3 CUP FLOUR
> 1/2 TEASPOON SALT
> 1/2 TEASPOON PEPPER
> 1/4 CUP CHOPPED FRESH CHIVES
> 1/4 CUP UNSALTED BUTTER, MELTED
> 2 LARGE EGGS
> 2 LARGE EGG YOLKS
> 1/2 CUP CLARIFIED UNSALTED BUTTER
> ABOUT 1 CUP CRÈME FRAÎCHE
> ASSORTED CAVIARS (SEVRUGA, GOLDEN WHITEFISH,
>   SALMON ROE—AS MUCH AS YOUR BUDGET WILL ALLOW)

Roughly chop the corn kernels, or pulse in a food processor until they have a chunky but creamy consistency. Place the corn in a large bowl and whisk in the milk, cornmeal, and flour, making sure there are no lumps. Season with salt and pepper and stir in 2 tablespoons of the chives.

In a separate bowl, whisk together the melted butter, whole eggs, and egg yolks.

In a large sauté pan over medium heat, heat the clarified butter. Ladle batter into the pan to make very small cakes, about the size of silver dollars. Cook for 2 minutes or until golden brown, then flip. Cook for an additional 2 minutes. Remove from the pan using a slotted spatula; place 4 corn cakes on each plate and repeat.

Garnish each plate of cakes with a dollop of crème fraîche and a generous sprinkling of the assorted caviars.

"Those who do not enjoy eating seldom have much
capacity for enjoyment of any sort."
—CHARLES WILLIAM ELLIOT, *The Happy Life*

SOUTHWESTERN CAESAR SALAD WITH JALAPEÑO-POLENTA CROUTONS

Kevin Rathbone, Chamyo, Atlanta, GA

Back in 1924, Caesar Cardini was running a popular restaurant in Tijuana, Mexico. Running low on food one night, he rummaged through his inventory and came up with the salad that forever after has borne his name. Serves 4.

CAESAR DRESSING

4 ANCHOVY FILLETS
1 TAMARIND POD, SEEDED AND MEAT REMOVED
JUICE OF 2 LIMES
4 CLOVES GARLIC, ROASTED
2 TEASPOONS BALSAMIC VINEGAR
2 EGG YOLKS
3/4 CUP DIJON MUSTARD
1 CUP VEGETABLE OIL
1/4 TEASPOON SALT
PINCH WHITE PEPPER
1/4 TEASPOON GROUND CUMIN

CROUTONS

2 CUPS WATER
1 TEASPOON SALT
1 JALAPEÑO, MINCED
1 1/4 CUPS CORNMEAL
2 CUPS VEGETABLE OIL FOR FRYING

1 HEAD ROMAINE LETTUCE, CLEANED AND BROKEN INTO
  LARGE PIECES
1/4 CUP GOOD-QUALITY SHAVED PARMESAN CHEESE
CAESAR DRESSING
2 CUPS FRIED CROUTONS

Make the dressing: In a food processor or blender, process the anchovies, tamarind, lime juice, garlic, vinegar, egg yolks, and mustard until smooth. Add the oil in a slow, steady stream until incorporated. Season with salt, pepper, and cumin. Set aside.

Make the croutons: In a saucepot, bring the water, salt, and jalapeño to a boil over high heat. Add 1 cup of the cornmeal, reduce heat to medium, and stir constantly for 5 minutes. Spoon the mixture onto a well-oiled baking sheet so that it is about 1/2 inch thick. Chill until firm, then dice into 1/2-inch cubes. Dust the cubes with the remaining cornmeal. In a large sauté pan, heat the oil over medium heat until hot but not smoking. Add a single layer of croutons and fry until golden, about 3 minutes. Repeat with remaining croutons.

Assemble the salad: In a large bowl, combine the lettuce, cheese, and croutons. Pour about 1 cup of the Caesar dressing over the greens, toss well, and serve immediately.

SILKY WHITE GAZPACHO WITH GRAPES AND TOASTED ALMONDS

The Blue Room, Cambridge, MA

Gazpacho actually started out in Spain many years ago as a soup composed largely of bread, garlic, and olive oil. Here the Blue Room's Lisa White creates a smooth and silky modern-day rendition that harks back to its early ancestors, with green grapes providing little bursts of sweetness, toasted almonds a nice crunch, and garlic a depth of flavor.

Actually, the high proportion of garlic in this soup might add another dimension to the dinner as well. This pungent bulb has been considered a potent aphrodisiac for centuries. According to an ancient Talmudic tradition garlic was believed to arouse sexual passion to such a degree that men were forbidden to eat it on the Sabbath. Serves 4 to 6.

> 1/2 LOAF (ABOUT 6 SLICES) FIRM WHITE BREAD, CRUSTS
>   REMOVED
> 5 CUCUMBERS, PEELED, SEEDED, AND ROUGHLY CHOPPED
> 4 TABLESPOONS MINCED GARLIC
> 3/4 CUP PURE OLIVE OIL
> 2 TABLESPOONS EXTRA VIRGIN OLIVE OIL
> 1/4 CUP SHERRY VINEGAR
> 1 TEASPOON KOSHER SALT OR 1/2 TEASPOON TABLE SALT
> 1 CUP SEEDLESS GREEN GRAPES, HALVED
> 2 TABLESPOONS GROUND TOASTED ALMONDS

Rip bread into large chunks, cover with cold water, and soak for 1 hour.

Meanwhile, combine the cucumbers, garlic, olive oil, vinegar, and salt in the bowl of a food processor or blender. Squeeze the water out of the bread with your hands and add to other ingredients. Blend until smooth. Cover and refrigerate for at least 1 hour. Just before serving, stir in grapes, garnish with toasted almonds, and serve.

POTENT PAPAYA CEVICHE

Curvaceous in shape, musky in fragrance, its dusky yellow or pink flesh centered with a core of black, shiny seeds, the papaya is among the world's most sensuous fruits. In many countries, slices of this aromatic fruit are eaten as a snack with just a squeeze of lime, perhaps because it is said to have the power to simultaneously tame an upset stomach and inflame passions.

In this rather unusual dish, oysters, scallops, and shrimp are cooked by lime juice, then tossed with avocado and the musky papaya. Jalapeño peppers provide heat while cilantro perfumes the whole affair, creating flavorful stimulation. Serves 6 to 8.

12 OYSTERS, SHUCKED
1 POUND SHRIMP, SHELLED AND DEVEINED
1 POUND SEA SCALLOPS, CUT INTO $1/4$-INCH DICE
1 CUP FRESH LIME JUICE PLUS 2 LIMES, WHOLE
1 TABLESPOON MINCED GARLIC
1 JALAPEÑO PEPPER, FINELY DICED
$1/4$ CUP OLIVE OIL
1 RIPE AVOCADO, PITTED, PEELED AND CUT INTO
    $1/4$-INCH DICE
1 PAPAYA, PITTED, PEELED, AND CUT INTO $1/4$-INCH DICE
4 ROMA TOMATOES, PEELED AND CUT INTO $1/4$-INCH DICE
3 TABLESPOONS CHOPPED FRESH CILANTRO

Place the oysters, shrimp, and scallops in a glass bowl and pour the lime juice and garlic over the mixture. Cover tightly and place in the refrigerator overnight, stirring once or twice.

Drain the seafood, toss with the jalapeño, olive oil, avocado, papaya, tomatoes, and cilantro. Squeeze the two limes over the mixture. Mix again and serve, accompanied by blue-corn tortilla chips.

LUSH PEACH SOUP

The Four Seasons, New York, NY

With its sweet, juice-filled fruit, its silken fuzzy exterior, and its full round shape, the peach has long been a symbol of ripe sexuality. Nicholas Culpepper, a seventeenth-century herbalist, wrote that "Venus owns this tree . . . the fruit provokes lust," and Arabs, Chinese, and Americans have all used "peach" as a symbol of a young woman.

Lush peaches, cinnamon and cloves for spice, and wine and brandy for a heady lift make this cold soup an ideal light beginning to a romantic meal. Serves 4.

> 6 RIPE PEACHES, PEELED AND PITTED
> 1 SMALL ORANGE, HALVED AND SEEDS REMOVED
> 1/2 LEMON, SEEDS REMOVED
> 1 BAY LEAF
> 1 CINNAMON STICK (YOU MAY SUBSTITUTE 1 TEASPOON
>   GROUND CINNAMON)
> 4 WHOLE CLOVES
> 2 CUPS DRY WHITE WINE
> 2 CUPS WATER
> 1/3 CUP SUGAR
> 1 TEASPOON CORNSTARCH
> 3 TABLESPOONS PEACH BRANDY
> 7 OUNCES GINGER ALE

Place the peaches, orange, and lemon in a large saucepan and add the bay leaf, cinnamon, cloves, wine, water, and sugar. Bring to a boil over medium heat. Reduce the heat slightly and simmer for 1 hour, or until all the ingredients are very tender.

In a small bowl, whisk the cornstarch into brandy. Stir the brandy into the peach mixture and return to a boil. Remove from the heat and allow to cool. Remove and discard the orange and lemon rinds, bay leaf, cinnamon stick, and cloves. Purée the mixture in a blender or food processor until smooth.

Push the mixture through a fine sieve into a bowl. Divide 1 cup of the soup into 4 small ramekins and freeze. Chill the rest of the soup and add ginger ale just before serving. Serve in chilled bowls and float frozen fruit on top.

"Give me women as soft and as delicate and as velvet as my peaches."

—OUIDA

TITILLATING TORTILLA SOUP

Adapted from The Inn of the Anasazi, Santa Fe, NM

This tasty soup is found in various guises all over Mexico and the American Southwest. You can basically use whatever vegetables or meats you have available, as long as crisp tortilla strips are part of the mix. Also, make sure you use plenty of garlic and onions, both of which were at one time banned in India because they were too stimulating. Serves 4 to 6 as a hearty appetizer.

1/2 CUP VEGETABLE OIL

8 CORN TORTILLAS, CUT INTO STRIPS

1 JALAPEÑO, SEEDED AND ROUGHLY CHOPPED

2 YELLOW ONIONS, CUT IN MEDIUM DICE

4 CLOVES GARLIC, ROUGHLY CHOPPED

12 CUPS CHICKEN STOCK, PREFERABLY HOMEMADE

8 OUNCES TOMATO JUICE

1 TABLESPOON TOMATO PASTE

2 TABLESPOONS GROUND CUMIN

1 TABLESPOON GROUND CORIANDER

1 TEASPOON GROUND RED PEPPER (CAYENNE)

1 RED BELL PEPPER, SEEDED AND SLICED VERY THIN

2 AVOCADOS, PEELED, PITTED, AND DICED

1 CUP COARSELY GRATED CHEDDAR CHEESE

ABOUT 1 CUP FRESH CILANTRO LEAVES

1 CUP GRILLED AND COOLED CHICKEN MEAT (OPTIONAL)

In a large stockpot, heat the oil over medium heat until hot but not smoking. Add the tortilla strips and fry until just golden brown and slightly crisp, about 3 minutes. Remove, drain on paper towels, and set aside.

Add the jalapeño, onions, and garlic to the pot and sauté, stirring occasionally, for about 5 minutes, or until the onions are transparent.

Add the chicken stock and tomato juice and bring to a boil. Add the tomato paste, cumin, coriander, and cayenne, turn the heat to low, and simmer for 30 minutes. Stir in the bell pepper and simmer for an additional 30 minutes.

Put about 2 tablespoons of grated cheese in the bottom of each individual serving bowl. Ladle the soup into the bowls and top each bowl with 4 or 5 tortilla strips, a handful of avocado, a sprinkling of cilantro leaves, and several pieces of chicken if desired.

"Tell me what you eat and I shall tell you what you are."
—ANTHELME BRILLAT-SAVARIN

SPICY CRAB SOUP

Adapted from Authentic Mexican *by Rick and Deann Bayless*

Shot through with the vibrant flavors of Mexico, this soup evokes the true pleasures of the kitchen. Roasting the garlic and tomatoes adds an extra richness to the base, as does the presence of chipotle peppers, which are dried smoked jalapeños. Along with corn and beans, fiery chile peppers were one of the "magic foods" of pre-Columbian Mexico. Of course, it also doesn't hurt that capsaicin, the component that makes chile peppers burn your mouth, is said to heat up desire as well. Letting your guests suck the meat out of the crab claws also provides a sensuous start to the meal. Serves 4 to 6 as a starter.

3 CLOVES GARLIC, UNPEELED
2 MEDIUM-SIZED TOMATOES
1/2 SMALL ONION, ROUGHLY CHOPPED
2 TABLESPOONS OLIVE OIL
2 QUARTS FISH STOCK
1 LARGE SPRIG EPAZOTE OR SEVERAL SPRIGS FLAT-LEAF PARSLEY
1 OR 2 CANNED CHIPOTLE CHILES, SEEDED AND CHOPPED
1/2 TEASPOON SALT
6 OUNCES CRABMEAT PLUS 4 CRAB LEGS, CRACKED
2 LIMES, CUT INTO WEDGES

Place the garlic and tomatoes in a nonstick skillet or foil-lined cast iron skillet and roast over medium heat, turning frequently, until the tomatoes are soft and their skin blistered, and the garlic cloves are soft and blackened in spots, about 15 minutes. Allow to cool. Push the softened garlic cloves out of their skins, core and peel the tomatoes, and place both in a blender or food processor along with the onions. Purée until smooth.

In a heavy soup pot, heat the olive oil over medium-high heat until a drop of the purée sizzles sharply when dropped into the oil. Add the purée all at once and stir constantly for 4 minutes; you want the purée to thicken and sear, but not to burn. Add the fish stock and the epazote or parsley, cover, and simmer over medium-low heat for 30 minutes.

About 15 minutes before serving, remove the epazote or parsley, skim off any fat floating on the surface, and stir in the chipotles and salt. Add the crabmeat and legs, cover, and allow to cook for about 5 minutes. Ladle into bowls, making sure that each person gets a crab leg, and pass lime wedges for people to squeeze into the soup.

ROASTED CORN AND BELL PEPPER SOUP

Mercury Bar, Boston, MA

Every spice used in this richly flavorful, Mexican-inspired soup is reputed to stimulate desire. Anchoring all of this wildness is corn, the bedrock staple of Mexican cuisine. It appears here both fresh and in the form of masa harina, a flour made from dried corn treated with slaked lime. To add earthiness, chef Steve Johnson uses even the corncobs to enrich the taste of the broth. Serves 6 to 8 as a starter.

4 EARS CORN, SHUCKED
1 RED BELL PEPPER
2 TABLESPOONS CORN OIL
1 ONION, DICED
1 RIB CELERY, DICED
4 CLOVES GARLIC, MINCED
1/2 TEASPOON GROUND CUMIN
1/2 TEASPOON GROUND CORIANDER
1/4 TEASPOON PAPRIKA
1/8 TEASPOON GROUND RED PEPPER (CAYENNE)
1 CINNAMON STICK (YOU MAY SUBSTITUTE 1 TEASPOON GROUND CINNAMON)
1 ANCHO PEPPER, STEMMED, SEEDED, AND MINCED
1 QUART CHICKEN STOCK
2 QUARTS WATER
SALT AND FRESHLY GROUND PEPPER TO TASTE
1 CUP MASA HARINA

GARNISH

1/2 CUP SOUR CREAM
1 FRESH TOMATO, DICED
2 TABLESPOONS CHOPPED CILANTRO

Over a medium fire, grill the corn until it has some color on all sides, about 6 to 8 minutes. As soon as the corn is cool enough to handle, slice off the kernels and set aside. Reserve the corncobs.

Meanwhile, roast the red bell pepper over the fire until the skin is completely black on all sides. Remove from the fire and allow to rest for 5 minutes in a paper bag. Rub off all the blackened skin, then seed, stem, and dice the pepper. Reserve with the corn kernels.

In a small stockpot, heat the oil over medium heat until hot but not smoking. Add the onion and celery and sauté until translucent, about 3 minutes. Add the garlic, cumin, coriander, paprika, cayenne, cinnamon, and ancho pepper and sauté, stirring, for another minute. Add the reserved corn cobs, chicken stock, 6 cups of the water, and salt and pepper to taste. Bring to a boil, then reduce the heat to low and simmer for 45 minutes. Remove and discard the corncobs and cinnamon stick.

In a small bowl, whisk together the remaining 2 cups of water with the masa harina. Add to the soup, whisking constantly as you do so to avoid lumps. Continue to simmer for an additional 30 minutes, stirring occasionally. Add the reserved corn and roasted pepper, cook for an additional 5 minutes, and check the seasoning. Serve garnished with sour cream, chopped tomato, and cilantro.

We may live without poetry, music, and art;
We may live without conscience,
and live without heart;
We may live without friends,
we may live without books;
But civilized man
cannot live without cooks.

—Owen Meredith
(Edward R. Bulwer-Lytton)

✣ENTRÉES✣

SEA BASS WITH CHAMPAGNE AND GRAPES

Ann Swain Catering, Houston, TX

Jonathan Swift claimed that fish, in order to taste its best, must swim three times: once in water, once in butter, once in wine. Here we forgo the butter, but to make up for that we use Champagne as the wine. Herbs, grapes, and nuts complete the aphrodisiac elements in this elegant treatment of firm-fleshed, sweet-tasting sea bass. Serves 4.

4 (8-OUNCE) SEA BASS FILLETS
SALT AND WHITE PEPPER TO TASTE
2/3 CUP DRY CHAMPAGNE
2 TABLESPOONS FRESH LEMON JUICE
3 SHALLOTS, MINCED
1/2 TEASPOON FINELY GRATED LEMON RIND
1/2 CUP LIGHT CREAM
2 TEASPOONS CHOPPED FRESH TARRAGON
1 CUP CHAMPAGNE GRAPES OR SEEDLESS GREEN GRAPES, HALVED
2 TABLESPOONS HAZELNUTS, FINELY CHOPPED
1 TABLESPOON CHOPPED FRESH CHIVES

Sprinkle the fillets with salt and pepper to taste and place in a medium-sized skillet. In a small bowl, combine the Champagne, lemon juice, shallots, and lemon peel. Pour this mixture over the fillets, bring to a boil over medium heat, reduce the heat to medium-low, cover, and simmer for 5 minutes. Remove the fish with a slotted spoon or spatula and transfer to a shallow glass baking dish.

Turn the heat to high and reduce the liquid in the skillet by about half. Remove from the heat, add the cream, and whisk together until smooth. Pour over the fish and top with grapes and hazelnuts. Place under the broiler for 2 to 3 minutes, garnish with fresh chives, and serve.

SAFFRON-SCENTED SHELLFISH STEW

Ivana Lowell

The rarer and more expensive a foodstuff, the more intense its aphrodisiac qualities are thought to be. Using that yardstick, saffron should cause virtual paroxysms of passion, since it reigns as the world's most costly spice. This aromatic spice is composed of the stigmas of a particular type of crocus, and to get a single pound of the spice, up to 250,000 of these stigmas must be picked by hand. Here saffron perfumes a quick, healthful shellfish stew. Serves 4.

1 1/2 POUNDS MUSSELS
1 1/2 POUNDS LITTLENECK CLAMS
2 CUPS CLAM JUICE
1 CUP WATER
1 CUP DRY WHITE WINE
3 CLOVES GARLIC, MINCED
1 TABLESPOON MINCED FRESH GINGERROOT
1 TEASPOON GRATED LEMON RIND
2 RIPE TOMATOES, DICED
1 BUNCH SCALLIONS, GREEN PART ONLY, MINCED
GENEROUS PINCH OF SAFFRON
2 TABLESPOONS OLIVE OIL
2 TABLESPOONS CHOPPED FRESH CILANTRO

Scrub clams and mussels very well in cold water, removing beards from the mussels. Discard any shellfish that are even partially open.

In a large pot, combine the clam juice, water, wine, garlic, ginger, and lemon rind and bring to a boil. Reduce the heat to medium-low and simmer for 10 minutes.

Add the clams, mussels, tomatoes, scallions, saffron, and oil. Bring the mixture back to a boil, remove from the heat, cover, and steep for 5 to 6 minutes or until clams and mussels have all opened. Garnish with cilantro and serve.

GRILLED RED SNAPPER WITH CILANTRO-LIME VINAIGRETTE

Ann Swain Catering, Houston, TX

Herbs and spices have always been thought of as aphrodisiacs. This belief became particularly strong in Europe during the dour Middle Ages, when pleasure of any kind was suspect. Since expensive herbs and spices were used solely to please the taste buds rather than to provide nutrition, they were considered frivolous, and therefore were suspected to stimulate lust and other evils of the flesh. Here the herb that stimulates is aromatic cilantro, which is very popular in Mexican and Southwestern cooking. It matches up particularly well with red snapper, one of northern Mexico's most popular fish. Serves 4.

4 (8-OUNCE) RED SNAPPER FILLETS
2 TABLESPOONS VEGETABLE OIL
1/4 CUP FRESH ORANGE JUICE
3 CLOVES GARLIC, MINCED
1/2 BUNCH CILANTRO, CLEANED AND CHOPPED
LIME ROUNDS FOR GARNISH (OPTIONAL)

VINAIGRETTE

2 TABLESPOONS FRESH LIME JUICE
2 TABLESPOONS WHITE WINE VINEGAR
2 TABLESPOONS RICE WINE VINEGAR
2 TABLESPOONS MINCED RED ONION
1 CLOVE GARLIC, MINCED
2 TABLESPOONS FINELY CHOPPED CILANTRO
2 SHALLOTS, MINCED
1/2 CUP PEANUT OIL
2 EARS CORN, SHUCKED, BOILED, AND KERNELS REMOVED
SALT AND FRESHLY GROUND PEPPER
2 LIMES, SLICED (OPTIONAL)

Place the fillets in a shallow dish. In a small bowl, combine the vegetable oil, orange juice, garlic, and cilantro. Pour over the snapper, cover, and refrigerate for 2 hours.

Meanwhile, make the vinaigrette: In a small bowl, combine the lime juice, white wine vinegar, rice wine vinegar, red onion, garlic, cilantro, and shallots. In a steady stream, whisk in the peanut oil. Stir in salt and pepper to taste. Stir in corn immediately before serving.

Preheat the broiler. Remove the snapper from marinade, discard the marinade, and transfer the fillets to a lightly oiled broiler pan. Broil until they are just translucent throughout, about 4 minutes per side.

To serve, place the snapper on serving plates and ladle a small amount of vinaigrette over the top. Garnish with lime rounds if desired.

"When you fish for love, bait with your heart not your brain."
—MARK TWAIN

SAUTÉED TROUT STUFFED WITH GARLIC, CHILE, AND TOASTED PECANS

Adapted from Big Flavors of the Hot Sun
by Chris Schlesinger and John Willoughby

Trout is a sweet and supple fish, as cleanly delicious as anything that dwells in the water. It is also the perfect size for serving whole to a single person, a presentation that always smacks of luxury and sensuous banquets. Enhanced with a stuffing of heady garlic, piquant chiles, and rich toasted pecans, the fish is then topped with a tart and herbaceous fresh tomato relish for a true feast of flavors. Serves 4.

RELISH

3 LARGE GARDEN TOMATOES, STEMMED AND CHOPPED FINE
1 SMALL RED ONION, CHOPPED FINE
1 TABLESPOON MINCED GARLIC
2 TABLESPOONS FRESH LIME JUICE
3 TABLESPOONS CHOPPED FRESH PARSLEY
2 TABLESPOONS VIRGIN OLIVE OIL
SALT AND FRESHLY GROUND BLACK PEPPER TO TASTE

4 (12-OUNCE) TROUT, CLEANED AND TOTALLY BONED
   OR SEMI-BONED WITH HEAD AND TAIL LEFT ON
2 TABLESPOONS VIRGIN OLIVE OIL
1 TABLESPOON MINCED GARLIC
2 TABLESPOONS MINCED RED OR GREEN CHILE PEPPER
2 TABLESPOONS CHOPPED FRESH CILANTRO
1/4 CUP PECANS, TOASTED AT 400°F FOR 4 MINUTES,
   ROUGHLY CHOPPED
1/2 CUP ALL-PURPOSE FLOUR
SALT AND FRESHLY GROUND BLACK PEPPER TO TASTE
1/4 CUP VIRGIN OLIVE OIL

In a medium-sized bowl, combine all the relish ingredients and mix well. Set aside. (May be kept, covered and refrigerated, for 3 days.)

Place the trout on a work surface. Combine the olive oil, garlic, chile, cilantro, and pecans. Spread the trout open and stuff one quarter of this mixture into the cavities.

In a large bowl or baking pan, mix the flour and salt and pepper well. Dredge the trout lightly in this flour mixture, shaking off any excess.

In your largest sauté pan, heat the oil over medium heat until hot but not smoking. Place the trout gently in the pan, turn the heat up to medium-high, and cook for 4 to 5 minutes per side or until golden brown and opaque throughout. Remove the trout from the pan and serve topped with a generous helping of the tomato relish.

"Show me another pleasure like dinner which comes every day and lasts an hour."

—TALLEYRAND

*L*SPICE-MASSAGED TUNA IN BED WITH GREENS

Cafe Pasqual's, Santa Fe, NM

Apicius, one of ancient Rome's most renowned gourmets, singled out tuna as a particularly effective "food of love." To add to its inherent appeal, this steaklike fish is coated with a spicy rub featuring chipotles (dried smoked jalapeño peppers), then combined with lushly sweet mangoes, crunchy jicama, and baby greens in a healthful dish guaranteed to stimulate all kinds of appetites. Serves 6.

RED CHILE PINE NUTS

> 1 CUP PINE NUTS
> 1/4 CUP WATER
> 2 TABLESPOONS SUGAR
> 3 TABLESPOONS CHILI POWDER

CHILE RUB

> 1/4 CUP CRACKED BLACK PEPPER
> 1/4 CUP BAY LEAVES
> 3 DRIED CHIPOTLE CHILES, DESTEMMED
> 2 TABLESPOONS HOT RED PEPPER FLAKES
> 1 TABLESPOON KOSHER SALT

VINAIGRETTE

> 1 TABLESPOON FRESH GINGERROOT, PEELED AND GRATED
> 2 LARGE SHALLOTS, MINCED
> 1/2 CUP RICE WINE VINEGAR
> 1 CUP PEANUT OIL
> 1 TABLESPOON ASIAN SESAME OIL
> 1/4 CUP FINELY MINCED FRESH GREEN CHILE
> SALT TO TASTE

1 POUND TUNA STEAK, TRIMMED OF SKIN

1 TABLESPOON OLIVE OIL

1 POUND MIXED TENDER GREENS (ARUGULA, SPINACH, OAK
   LEAF LETTUCE, WATERCRESS, DANDELION, BUTTER LETTUCE,
   MUSTARD, ETC.), WELL WASHED AND DRIED

2 RIPE MANGOES, PITTED, PEELED, AND CUT INTO THIN SLICES

1 SMALL JICAMA, PEELED AND CUT INTO MATCHSTICKS

To prepare the pine nuts: Preheat the oven to 350°F. Spread the pine nuts on a baking sheet and toast in the oven for 5 to 7 minutes. Remove from the oven and place the nuts in a small bowl. Add the water, sugar, and chili powder and toss to mix well. Spread the nuts on the baking sheet and return to the oven for 5 to 7 minutes. Remove and set aside to cool.

To prepare the chile rub: In a small bowl, combine the black pepper, bay leaves, chipotles, pepper flakes, and salt and grind coarsely in a spice grinder, coffee grinder, or mortar and pestle. Set aside.

To prepare the vinaigrette: Squeeze the juice from the fresh ginger into a mixing bowl and discard the pulp. Add the shallots, vinegar, peanut oil, sesame oil, and chile and blend well. Add salt to taste. The vinaigrette may be prepared several days in advance.

To cook the tuna: Rub the tuna on all sides first with the olive oil and then with the chile rub. Grill over a medium-hot fire for about 3 minutes on each side for rare; check the doneness and cook longer if desired, but be careful not to overcook. Slice the grilled tuna into slices about 1/4 inch thick.

To assemble the salad: Toss the greens with the vinaigrette in a large mixing bowl. Arrange the greens in the center of each plate. Arrange the tuna slices, mango slices, and jicama on the greens in an alternating and radiating pattern. Sprinkle with toasted pine nuts.

SCALLOPS WITH CILANTRO
AND SAFFRON COCONUT CREAM

Adapted from Fish: Complete Guide to Buying and Cooking *by Mark Bittman*

Serves 4.

> 1 CUP UNSWEETENED SHREDDED DRIED COCONUT
> 1/8 TEASPOON SAFFRON
> 2 CUPS BOILING WATER
> 3 TABLESPOONS VEGETABLE OIL
> 1 LARGE ONION, HALVED AND SLICED THIN
> 1 TABLESPOON MINCED FRESH GINGERROOT
> 1 TEASPOON MINCED GARLIC
> 1 TEASPOON SALT
> 1/4 TEASPOON GROUND RED PEPPER (CAYENNE)
> 1/2 CUP MINCED FRESH CILANTRO
> 1 POUND SEA SCALLOPS, HALVED IF VERY LARGE
> 2 PLUM TOMATOES, HALVED, SEEDED, AND DICED
> SALT TO TASTE

In a blender, combine the coconut, saffron, and boiling water. Blend for 15 seconds, allow the liquid to stand for 10 minutes, then pour through a fine strainer into a bowl. Set the coconut milk aside.

Heat the oil in a skillet over medium heat. Add the onion and cook, stirring, until translucent, about 5 to 7 minutes. Lower the heat to medium-low, add the ginger, garlic, salt, and cayenne, and cook for 5 minutes, stirring constantly. Add 1 1/2 cups of the coconut milk, raise the heat to medium, and bring to a gentle boil. Add 1/4 cup of the cilantro and cook, stirring occasionally, until the sauce is slightly reduced, 5 to 10 minutes.

Add the scallops and tomatoes to the sauce and cook, stirring occasionally, until the scallops are almost completely translucent, about 4 minutes. Remove from the heat, add the remaining 1/4 cup of cilantro, season to taste, and serve.

An Appetite for Passion

SKEWERED OYSTERS AND JALAPEÑOS

Adapted from Galatoires, New Orleans, LA

In the realm of aphrodisiac foods, oysters are king—or queen. Certain varieties of these switch-hitting bivalves actually change from male to female with each successive reproductive cycle. With this wealth of experience, it is perhaps no wonder that they are the most well-known aphrodisiac food in the world. Here they are combined with bacon and jalapeños on a brochette that can make an easy and unusual appetizer as well as a main course. Serves 2.

12 STRIPS OF BACON, HALVED AND FRIED UNTIL BARELY CRISP
2 DOZEN RAW OYSTERS
6 JALAPEÑOS, CUT IN QUARTERS LENGTHWISE AND SEEDED
SALT AND FRESHLY GROUND PEPPER TO TASTE
1 EGG
3/4 CUP MILK
1/2 CUP FLOUR
3 CUPS VEGETABLE OIL FOR FRYING
LEMON WEDGES FOR GARNISH

Thread the bacon, oysters, and jalapeño quarters alternately onto 8 short wooden or metal skewers. Sprinkle with salt and pepper.

In a small wide bowl, whisk together the egg and milk.

In a large deep sauté pan, heat the oil over medium heat until hot but not smoking. Dip each skewer into the egg milk batter, roll in flour, shake off excess flour, and fry in the hot oil until just golden, about 5 minutes. Serve garnished with lemon wedges.

> **"Oysters are more beautiful than any religion. There's nothing in Christianity or Buddhism that quite matches the sympathetic unselfishness of the oyster."**
>
> —SAKI

MARINATED SALMON WITH WARM LEEK-GINGER VINAIGRETTE

Eugenia Citkowitz, Los Angles, CA. An English brainy beauty who can be found climbing Africa's mountains or writing in Los Angeles, Citkowitz often serves this delicate dish to her husband, actor Julian Sands.

Pungent, highly aromatic, and imbued with the mystery of the East, ginger is considered the most powerful aphrodisiac among spices. Extremely popular in medieval Europe, it was also coveted in Africa and China as a means of ensuring many children. So prized was ginger in Arab cultures that, according to the Koran, virtuous Muslims in Paradise will be served with "goblets of ginger-flavored water." No need to wait for Paradise, however; here ginger, leeks, and orange flavor a light, healthful salmon dish. Serves 4.

4 (8-OUNCE) SALMON FILLETS
SALT AND FRESHLY GROUND PEPPER TO TASTE
2 TABLESPOONS MINCED FRESH GINGER
3 CLOVES GARLIC, MINCED
2 TABLESPOONS LIGHT SOY SAUCE
1/4 CUP FRESH ORANGE JUICE
1/4 CUP OLIVE OIL
2 TABLESPOONS BROWN SUGAR

VINAIGRETTE

2 TABLESPOONS MINCED LEEKS
2 SHALLOTS, MINCED
1 TABLESPOON GRATED FRESH GINGER
1 TABLESPOON MINCED CILANTRO OR PARSLEY
1/4 CUP FRESH LIME JUICE
2 TABLESPOONS APPLE CIDER VINEGAR
2 TEASPOONS LIGHT SOY SAUCE
1/2 CUP VEGETABLE OIL
SALT AND FRESHLY GROUND PEPPER TO TASTE

Sprinkle the salmon with salt and pepper and place in a shallow glass dish. In a small bowl, combine the ginger, garlic, soy sauce, orange juice, olive oil, and brown sugar. Mix well and pour over the fillets. Cover and refrigerate for 2 to 4 hours.

Just before you are ready to cook, make the vinaigrette: Combine the leeks, shallots, ginger, cilantro, lime juice, vinegar, and soy sauce in a small saucepan. Bring to a boil, reduce the heat to low, and simmer for 5 minutes. Remove from heat and whisk in the vegetable oil and salt and pepper to taste. Return to the stove over very low heat and keep warm but do not allow to boil.

Remove the salmon from the marinade and place under a preheated broiler until just cooked through, about 4 to 5 minutes per side. Place one fillet on each serving plate, drizzle each with a tablespoon of warm vinaigrette, and serve immediately.

**"Hot ginger quenches thirst, revives, excites the brain
And in old age awakens young love again."**
—REGIMAN SANITATIS SALERNO

SALMON CAKES WITH DILL-CAPER TARTAR SAUCE

Adapted from Wilton's, London, England

Salmon and other fish have always been considered foods of love. There is some evidence that the high phosphorus and iodine content of seafood may actually have some beneficial effect on sexual potency. All things considered, however, it is probably more important that Aphrodite, goddess of love, was said to have emerged full-grown from the sea, as if she herself were a water creature. After all, in matters of the heart, myth is definitely more powerful than science. Serves 4.

2 1/2 POUNDS SALMON FILLETS, SKINNED
1 CUP WATER
1 CUP WHITE WINE
1 POUND POTATOES
1 BUNCH CILANTRO, CLEANED AND CHOPPED
GENEROUS PINCH OF GROUND RED (CAYENNE) PEPPER, OR
   MORE TO TASTE
1 TABLESPOON FRESH HORSERADISH (YOU MAY SUBSTITUTE
   PREPARED HORSERADISH)
SALT AND FRESHLY GROUND PEPPER
2 EGGS
1/4 CUP WATER
1/2 CUP FLOUR
1 1/2 CUPS BREAD CRUMBS
3 CUPS VEGETABLE OIL

Arrange the salmon fillets in a large skillet and pour in the wine and water, making sure the fillets are covered. Bring the liquid to a boil over medium-high heat and cover the skillet. Reduce the heat to low and poach for about 8 minutes, or until the fish flakes easily when tested with a fork. Remove from the heat, drain, and cool.

Peel and cube the potatoes and cook in a pot of boiling salted water for 8 to 10 minutes or until easily pierced with a fork. Drain well and mash to a medium consistency.

Gently flake salmon into small pieces and transfer to a large bowl with the potatoes. Add the cilantro, cayenne, horseradish, and salt and pepper to taste. Gently mix with a fork and refrigerate until firm. Form into cakes about 2 inches in diameter.

Break the eggs into a shallow dish, add $1/4$ cup of water, and mix well. Place the flour in a second bowl along with a bit of salt and pepper, and place bread crumbs in a third bowl. Dredge the salmon cakes first in seasoned flour, then egg wash, then bread crumbs.

Heat the oil over medium heat in a deep heavy saucepan. Add the salmon cakes 3 or 4 at a time and fry until golden brown all over. Remove and drain on paper towels. Repeat until all salmon cakes are cooked. Serve with dill-caper tartar sauce (*below*).

DILL-CAPER TARTAR SAUCE

> 1 CUP LIGHT MAYONNAISE
> $1/4$ CUP MINCED SHALLOTS
> 2 TABLESPOONS MINCED CAPERS
> 1 TEASPOON DIJON MUSTARD
> 2 TABLESPOONS MINCED FRESH PARSLEY
> 2 TABLESPOONS MINCED FRESH DILL
> 2 TEASPOONS LEMON JUICE
> 1 HARD-BOILED EGG, FORCED THROUGH A COARSE SIEVE

Combine all the ingredients in a small bowl and mix well. Makes about $1^1/2$ cups.

PASTA WITH TEQUILA-SOAKED OYSTERS AND CAVIAR

Adapted from Caviarteria, New York

The Duc de Richelieu's elaborate banquets, where everyone ate in the nude, lavished such high-powered aphrodisiacs as oysters and marzipan. Serves 4.

3 SHALLOTS, MINCED
2 TEASPOONS FRESH LIME JUICE
1/2 CUP GOLD TEQUILA
2 TABLESPOONS UNSALTED BUTTER
2/3 CUP HEAVY CREAM
3 TABLESPOONS MINCED FRESH CHIVES
SALT AND FRESHLY GROUND PEPPER
2 DOZEN SHUCKED OYSTERS
12 OUNCES ANGEL HAIR PASTA
2 TABLESPOONS CAVIAR (SEVRUGA, BLACK OR RED LUMPFISH, OR WHATEVER YOUR BUDGET ALLOWS)
2 TABLESPOONS FINELY CHOPPED PARSLEY OR CILANTRO

Preheat the oven to 375°F. In a small saucepan over medium-high heat, combine the shallots, lime juice, and tequila. Bring to a boil, turn the heat to low, and simmer for 3 minutes. Add the butter and whisk until smooth. Whisk in the cream and simmer for 3 to 4 minutes, keeping the heat at low. Add the chives and salt and pepper to taste. Remove from the heat.

Rinse the oysters in cool water and pat dry. Place the oysters in a shallow glass baking dish, pour tequila-lime mixture over them, and bake for 5 to 7 minutes or until just firm. Note: The edges of the oysters will start to curl up when almost firm.

Meanwhile, cook the pasta al dente in boiling salted water and drain. Place one quarter of the pasta on each plate, top each serving with six oysters and sauce, and garnish with caviar and parsley.

HEDONISTIC HASH WITH TRUFFLES AND FOIE GRAS

Adapted from The Carlyle, New York, NY

Hash is usually a humble dish, but this version contains two of the world's most extravagant foods: truffles and foie gras. Meltingly rich foie gras, the liver of force-fed geese, was a favorite seductive tool of the legendary lover Casanova, and musky truffles have been prized as aphrodisiacs since the days of ancient Babylon. Serves 4.

> 4 BONELESS, SKINLESS, 6-OUNCE CHICKEN BREAST HALVES
> 1/2 POUND FRESH GOOSE OR DUCK LIVERS
> 2 TABLESPOONS OLIVE OIL
> 1/2 CUP HEAVY CREAM
> SALT AND FRESHLY GROUND PEPPER TO TASTE
> 1 BLACK TRUFFLE, FINELY JULIENNED
> 1 TABLESPOON CHOPPED FRESH CHIVES

Bring a small pot of water to boil. Add the chicken breasts, cover, reduce heat to low, and simmer until breasts are white throughout, about 10 to 12 minutes. Remove, cool, and cut into 2-inch pieces.

Dice the duck liver. In a small skillet, heat the olive oil over medium heat until hot but not smoking. Add the diced duck liver and sauté until lightly browned, 3 to 4 minutes. Add the diced chicken and heavy cream and cook until the volume is reduced by about half. Add salt and a generous amount of pepper, gently stir in truffles, and serve, garnished with chives.

PASTA WITH SHELLFISH MÉLANGE
Nan Kempner, New York, NY

Ultra-fashionable hostess Nan Kempner, who maintains a stylishly thin figure, is nevertheless renowned for her voracious appetite. An excellent chef, she has been known to finish not only the food on her own plate but that of her guests as well—and her guests include such luminaries as European royals and wives of American presidents.

Sharing a plate of this shellfish pasta might turn out to be particularly seductive, since basil is a primary ingredient. This aromatic herb was at the top of Ovid's list of aphrodisiac foods, and even today it is used in voodoo love ceremonies in Haiti, where it is associated with the sex goddess Erzulie. Serves 4 or 6.

2 ROCK LOBSTER TAILS
2¹/₂ POUNDS RIPE ROMA TOMATOES
2 TABLESPOONS OLIVE OIL
1 LARGE ONION, ROUGHLY CHOPPED
5 CLOVES GARLIC, MINCED
1 JALAPEÑO PEPPER, STEMMED AND SEEDS REMOVED
2 TABLESPOONS TOMATO PASTE
2 TABLESPOONS FRESH LIME JUICE
6 TABLESPOONS CHOPPED FRESH BASIL
SALT AND FRESHLY GROUND PEPPER TO TASTE
1 TABLESPOON BUTTER
¹/₂ POUND FRESH LUMP CRABMEAT, PICKED OVER WELL
6 LARGE COOKED SHRIMP, SHELLED AND SLICED IN HALF
12 OUNCES LINGUINI

Fill a large pot full of water and bring to a boil. Add the lobster tails and cook until just white throughout, about 5 to 8 minutes. Remove the lobster with tongs or a slotted spoon, leaving the water on the stove. As soon as the lobster is cool enough, cut each tail on the bias into 12 medallions. Set aside.

Meanwhile, cut an X on the top of each tomato and plunge into the boiling water for 30 seconds. Remove and run under cold water, slipping off the skins at the same time. Halve the tomatoes, remove the seeds, and reserve the tomatoes.

In a medium saucepan, heat 1 tablespoon of olive oil over medium heat until hot but not smoking. Add the onion, garlic, and jalapeño and sauté, stirring occasionally, until the onion is transparent, about 5 minutes. Add the reserved tomatoes and tomato paste and simmer for 10 minutes. Remove from the heat and purée in a food processor or blender. Add the lime juice, all but about 2 tablespoons of the basil, and the remaining tablespoon of olive oil. Season to taste.

In a small sauté pan, melt the butter over medium heat. Add the reserved lobster, the crabmeat, and the shrimp and sauté, stirring gently, until just warmed through, 4 to 5 minutes.

Meanwhile, cook the linguini al dente in a large pot of boiling salted water. Drain. Place some of the linguini in the center of each plate, top with a generous amount of the tomato sauce, and garnish with the shrimp, crabmeat, lobster medallions, and the remaining chopped basil.

"A good cook is like a sorcerer who dispenses happiness."
—ELSA SCHIAPARELLI

HEARTS OF PALM AND LOBSTER SALAD

Adapted from the Eastern Orient Express

Because it is low in calories, lobster salad has come to be considered a dish for "ladies who lunch." Maybe . . . but that may lead to some pretty wild afternoons, because this luxe crustacean was used as an aphrodisiac by everyone from the ancient Mayans to Suleiman the Magnificent. This particular salad continues that exotic tradition, since it is served on the lavish Eastern Orient Express, which winds its way from Singapore to Bangkok. Serves 4.

DILL VINAIGRETTE

3 TABLESPOONS WHITE WINE VINEGAR
1 TABLESPOON DIJON MUSTARD
3 SHALLOTS, CHOPPED FINE
1 TABLESPOON CHOPPED FRESH DILL
3/4 CUP OLIVE OIL
SALT AND FRESHLY GROUND PEPPER

4 ROCK LOBSTER TAILS
1 (16-OUNCE) CAN HEARTS OF PALM, DRAINED
3/4 POUND MIXED TENDER GREENS (ARUGULA, BIBB
   LETTUCE, RED LEAF LETTUCE, MÂCHE, DANDELION
   GREENS, ESCAROLE, ETC.)
1 (16-OUNCE) CAN MANDARIN ORANGES, DRAINED
1/4 RED ONION, SLICED VERY THIN

Make the vinaigrette: In a small bowl, whisk together the vinegar, mustard, shallots, dill, and olive oil. Season to taste.

Poach the lobster tails in simmering water to cover until just cooked through, about 5 to 8 minutes. Remove from the heat, chill, and slice each tail into 6 medallions. Meanwhile, cut the hearts of palm on the bias into pieces about 1/2 inch thick.

To assemble the salad, toss the mixed greens in a large bowl with the vinaigrette. Place the dressed greens in the center of 4 serving plates and spread the lobster medallions in a domino fashion at six o'clock. Garnish with hearts of palm, oranges, and red onion.

**"A woman should never be seen eating and drinking,
unless it be lobster salad and Champagne,
the only two feminine and becoming viands."**

—LORD BYRON

RECKLESS CHICKEN MOLE

Adapted from Food from My Heart *by Zarela Martinez*

Moles are to Mexican cooking what sauces of butter and cream are to
French. Intricate, subtle, intoxicating in flavor and aroma, these
complex combinations of spices, nuts, fruits, and bitter chocolate are
truly a love affair between cook and ingredients. Undertake this dish
when you want to lavish love and care on your cooking. As you do,
you may find that a kind of kitchen alchemy will transfer your
emotions to those who eat. Serves 6.

1/4 POUND ANCHO CHILES, STEMS AND TIPS REMOVED

1/4 POUND GUAJILLA CHILES, STEMS AND TIPS REMOVED

6 WHOLE BLACK PEPPERCORNS

3 WHOLE CLOVES

1/4-INCH PIECE OF STICK CINNAMON (OR 1 TEASPOON
    GROUND CINNAMON)

1 TABLESPOON DRIED MEXICAN OREGANO

ABOUT 1/2 CUP VEGETABLE OIL

1/4 CUP SESAME SEEDS

1/4 CUP DRY-ROASTED UNSALTED PEANUTS

1/4 CUP SLIVERED ALMONDS

1/4 CUP WALNUTS OR PECANS

1/4 CUP GOLDEN RAISINS

1/2 CUP PITTED PRUNES, ROUGHLY SLICED

1/2 CUP PITTED DRIED APRICOTS, ROUGHLY SLICED

3/4 CUP DRY SHERRY, HEATED

1 TABLESPOON BUTTER

1 SMALL, VERY RIPE PLANTAIN, PEELED AND CUT INTO
    1/2-INCH SLICES

5 CLOVES GARLIC, UNPEELED

1 ONION, UNPEELED

1 LARGE OR 2 MEDIUM-SIZED FIRM, RIPE TOMATOES

4 TO 5 CUPS CHICKEN STOCK

1/4 POUND FRESH TOMATILLOS, HUSKED

2 OUNCES MEXICAN CHOCOLATE, ROUGHLY CHOPPED
8 GRILLED OR BROILED BONELESS, SKINLESS CHICKEN
BREAST HALVES

First prepare the various sets of ingredients: Rinse the chiles under cold running water, removing seeds. Heat a cast iron skillet over high heat until a drop of water gives a lively sizzle on contact. A few at a time, briefly toast the chiles on the skillet, turning once or twice, just until their aroma is released, about 2 minutes each. Be very careful not to let them scorch. As the chiles are done, place in a large saucepan. Cover with boiling water and allow to soak until softened, 8 to 10 minutes, but no more. Drain and set the chiles aside.

Clean the skillet and place over medium-low heat. Add the peppercorns and cloves and toast, shaking the pan continuously, until their aroma is released. Toast the cinnamon stick and the oregano separately in the same pan until fragrant, about 2 minutes each. Combine all the spices and set aside.

Clean the skillet and heat 2 tablespoons of vegetable oil over medium heat until hot but not smoking. Add the sesame seeds and cook, stirring, until just golden, about 3 to 4 minutes. Remove the sesame seeds to a small bowl and sequentially cook the peanuts, almonds, and walnuts in the same manner, adding a bit of oil each time and removing each type of nuts to the bowl as toasted. Set aside.

Combine the raisins, prunes, and apricots in a bowl and pour the hot sherry over them. Set aside to soften.

In a small skillet, heat the butter over medium heat until melted. Add the plantain slices and cook, stirring, until golden on both sides, about 3 to 4 minutes. Set aside.

(continued on next page)

Heat the large cast-iron skillet over high heat until a drop of water gives a lively sizzle on contact. Put the garlic and onion on the skillet and roast, turning several times, until the onion is black on all sides and the garlic is dark and somewhat softened. Peel the onion and garlic and coarsely chop the peeled onion. Set aside. In the same skillet, roast the tomatoes, turning several times, until blackened on all sides. Place in a bowl, allow to cool, and slip off the skins.

Now begin puréeing ingredients in sequence: Place half the chiles, half the spices, and 1 cup of chicken stock in a blender or food processor and process until smooth. Repeat with the second half of the chiles and spices. Using a wooden spoon, force the puréed mixture through a sieve into a bowl and discard anything that does not go through. Scrape the purée into a large saucepan.

Rinse the blender or food processor and purée the sesame seeds, peanuts, almonds, and walnuts in several batches, using just enough chicken stock with each batch to produce a smooth paste. Add to the chile-spice mixture in the saucepan. Purée the dried fruit mixture, along with the sautéed plantain, in the same manner. Add to the saucepan. Purée the onion, garlic, tomatoes, and tomatillos in a similar manner (you may not need to add stock to them), in batches if necessary. Add to the saucepan along with the chocolate.

Bring the sauce to a boil over medium heat, stirring constantly. Reduce the heat to medium low, stir in 2 cups of chicken broth, and simmer, uncovered, stirring frequently, for 30 minutes. If necessary, add additional chicken broth during cooking to keep the sauce to the consistency of heavy cream.

Just before serving, add the chicken breasts to the sauce. When the breasts are heated through, about 5 minutes, remove them to a serving platter and spoon the sauce over them. Serve accompanied by additional sautéed sliced plantains.

SPICED ROAST CHICKEN

A whole, juicy roast chicken is the ultimate in comfort food. Not just for those who eat it, but also for the cook, since it takes so little time to prepare. By rubbing a mixture of typical Latin seasonings under the skin, you end up with a bird suffused with the spicy flavors of Latin American cookery. Serves 6.

1 ROASTING CHICKEN, 4 TO 5 POUNDS
2 TABLESPOONS GROUND CUMIN
2 TABLESPOONS CHILI POWDER
1 TABLESPOON CRUSHED CORIANDER SEEDS
1 TEASPOON GROUND CINNAMON
2 TABLESPOONS BROWN SUGAR
1 TEASPOON SALT
1 TEASPOON HOT RED PEPPER FLAKES
FRESHLY GROUND BLACK PEPPER
1/4 CUP UNSALTED BUTTER, MELTED

Preheat the oven to 400°F. In a small bowl, combine the cumin, chili powder, coriander, cinnamon, brown sugar, salt, hot pepper flakes, and black pepper. Mix well. Starting at the top of the breastbone, loosen the skin from the breast of the chicken, being careful not to tear the skin. Gently rub the spice mixture under the skin, making sure you work as far back and to the sides as possible. Sprinkle the outside of the chicken with salt and pepper to taste.

Place the chicken on a cooking rack set in a roasting pan. Roast in the preheated oven for about 30 minutes, brushing the exterior with melted butter every 10 minutes or so. Reduce the heat to 325° and continue roasting for an additional 30 minutes or until the juices run clear when you stick a fork into the thigh portion of the chicken. Remove from the oven, transfer to a platter, and allow to sit for 10 minutes before carving

SAUCY QUAIL WITH TOMATILLO SAUCE

Ann Swain Catering, Houston, TX

Quail are a wonderful romantic mix of the delicate, rich, and exotic. In this recipe, quail are bathed in a marinade combining Mexican and Asian flavors, then draped in a classic Southwestern tomatillo sauce. The mild but refreshing flavor of the tomatillos, which resemble small green tomatoes, complements the richness of the quail. Serves 4.

8 QUAIL, BONED
1/2 CUP FRESH LIME JUICE
1/4 CUP SOY SAUCE
2 TABLESPOONS MINCED GINGER
1 BUNCH CILANTRO, ROUGHLY CHOPPED
1 TABLESPOON MINCED GARLIC
1 TEASPOON HOT RED PEPPER FLAKES
1 TEASPOON FISH SAUCE (NAM PLA) (OPTIONAL)

Rinse the quail and pat them dry. Combine the lime juice, soy sauce, ginger, cilantro, garlic, hot pepper, and fish sauce and mix well. Pour over the quail, cover, and refrigerate; allow to stand for 6 to 12 hours, turning occasionally.

Preheat the oven to 425°F. Remove the quail from the marinade and arrange them breast side down in a large roasting pan. Place in the oven for 4 to 5 minutes, turn them, and roast for another 4 to 5 minutes or until they are no longer springy to the touch and their juices run clear when pierced. Serve draped with tomatillo sauce (*opposite*).

TOMATILLO SAUCE

2 TABLESPOONS OLIVE OIL
1 LARGE ONION, ROUGHLY CHOPPED
1 POUND FRESH TOMATILLOS, HUSKED
4 CLOVES GARLIC, PEELED
1 CUP CHICKEN STOCK
$1/2$ CUP SOUR CREAM
1 TABLESPOON FRESH LIME JUICE
$1/2$ BUNCH FRESH CILANTRO
$1/2$ ANAHEIM PEPPER, SEEDS REMOVED

In a small saucepan, heat the olive oil until hot but not smoking. Add the onion and sauté until translucent, about 5 minutes. Set aside.

In another saucepan, bring enough water to a boil to cover the tomatillos. When the water is boiling, add the tomatillos and poach until they turn to mustard green, about 10 to 12 minutes. Drain tomatillos and allow to cool to room temperature.

Put the tomatillos in a blender or food processor along with the sautéed onions and all the remaining sauce ingredients. Purée until smooth. Just before serving, return to the saucepan and warm over low heat.

"There are only two occasions when I drink Champagne,
and those are when I have game for dinner and when I haven't."
—S.D. CHURCHILL, a nineteenth-century wine merchant

GRILLED QUAIL BATHED IN BLOOD ORANGES

Adapted from Auberge du Soleil, Napa Valley, CA

When you sit down to the table, it seems indulgent to have a whole tiny bird to yourself. This sybaritic pleasure helps explain the appeal of quail as a special-occasion dish. Here the dramatically ruby-red juice of blood oranges makes a vinaigrette to match the exotic nature of these little birds. Serves 4.

VINAIGRETTE

1/2 CUP FRESH BLOOD ORANGE JUICE (YOU MAY SUBSTITUTE
    REGULAR ORANGE JUICE)
6 SHALLOTS, MINCED
1 TEASPOON CHOPPED FRESH THYME
1 TEASPOON CHOPPED FRESH MARJORAM
1/2 CUP OLIVE OIL
SALT AND FRESHLY GROUND BLACK PEPPER

8 QUAIL, BONED (ASK YOUR BUTCHER TO BONE THEM
    FOR YOU), RINSED, AND PATTED DRY
2 TABLESPOONS OLIVE OIL
SALT AND FRESHLY GROUND PEPPER TO TASTE

WILTED GREENS

2 TABLESPOONS OLIVE OIL
1 TEASPOON MINCED GARLIC
2 POUNDS SWISS CHARD OR OTHER TENDER GREENS,
    CLEANED AND DRIED
SALT AND FRESHLY GROUND PEPPER TO TASTE

Make the vinaigrette: In a blender or food processor, combine the orange juice, shallots, and olive oil and blend until smooth. Pour into a mixing bowl, fold in the thyme and marjoram, and season to taste with salt and pepper. Set aside.

Grill the quail: In a small bowl, toss the quail with the olive oil, salt, and pepper. Place quail on a grill over a medium-hot fire or under a preheated broiler and cook until the skin is crisp and golden, about 3 to 4 minutes per side. The birds should be cooked through, but still a little pinkish on the interior. Remove the quail from the heat and cut on the bias into four pieces each.

Cook the greens: In a large sauté pan, heat the olive oil over medium-high heat until hot but not smoking. Add the garlic and sauté, stirring, for 2 minutes. Add the greens and cook, stirring frequently, until the greens are wilted but still bright green, about 5 minutes. Season with salt and pepper.

Assemble the dish: Put one quarter of the greens on each plate, lay two of the sliced quail on top, and drizzle the whole liberally with the blood orange vinaigrette.

> **"A true gastronome should always be ready to eat, just as a soldier should always be ready to fight."**
> —Charles Monselet

$\mathcal{L}$BREAST OF DUCK WITH FRESH CHILES

Adapted from David Waltuck, Chanterelle, New York, NY

Chile peppers were unknown outside the Americas until after Columbus's voyage. It didn't take long, however, for them to spread around the world and become indispensable in cuisines from India to North Africa. Not only did they make the food more adventuresome; they were also reputed to make those who ate them sexually frisky. Here they add a bit of heat to a wine-tomato sauce served over rich duck breasts. Serves 4.

1 1/2 RED BELL PEPPERS, SEEDED
1 JALAPEÑO PEPPER, SEEDED
1/2 ANAHEIM PEPPER OR ANY MILD CHILE PEPPER, SEEDED
4 TABLESPOONS OLIVE OIL
2 CARROTS, PEELED AND CUT IN MEDIUM DICE
1 1/2 ONIONS, CUT IN MEDIUM DICE
4 CLOVES GARLIC, MINCED
1/3 CUP WHITE WINE
1/3 CUP SHERRY VINEGAR
1/2 CUP CANNED TOMATOES
2 CUPS BROWN DUCK STOCK (YOU MAY SUBSTITUTE
  CHICKEN STOCK)
4 BONELESS, SKINLESS DUCK BREAST HALVES

In a food processor or blender, combine the three peppers and chop fine. Set aside.

In a heavy saucepan, heat 2 tablespoons of olive oil over medium heat until hot but not smoking. Add the carrots, onions, and garlic and sauté, stirring, until the onions are transparent, 5 to 7 minutes. Add the wine and sherry vinegar and cook, stirring constantly, until almost dry. Add the tomatoes and stock, bring to a boil, reduce the heat to low, and simmer, stirring occasionally, for 45 minutes. Strain the mixture, return to the sauté pan, and add the reserved peppers. Bring the mixture to a boil, lower the heat slightly, and reduce by about half or until desired consistency is reached.

Meanwhile, in a medium skillet, heat the remaining 2 tablespoons of olive oil over medium heat until hot but not smoking. Add the duck breasts and sauté for 4 to 5 minutes per side, or until the interior retains just a trace of pink. Remove from the heat, slice on the bias, and serve immediately, topped with the sauce.

> "The genius of love and the genius of hunger
> are the two moving forces behind all living things."
> —TURGENEV, *Little Poems in Prose*

DRUNKEN DUCK IN BITTER ORANGE

Lisa Fine

The brilliant golden-orange exterior and sweet, juicy interior of oranges have made them a favorite of lovers through the centuries. Elegant courtesans used to sprinkle their bed sheets with orange water, and an ancient custom held that if lovers bathed in orange-scented water after the first time they made love, their love life would be a long and happy one. Here we bathe a roast duck in a sauce of bitter orange and brandy, providing at least a momentary happiness to those who eat it. Serves 2, generous portions.

1 (4–5 POUND) DUCK
SALT AND FRESHLY GROUND PEPPER TO TASTE
4 TEASPOONS GRATED BITTER ORANGE PEEL (YOU MAY
   SUBSTITUTE 3 TEASPOONS STANDARD ORANGE PEEL PLUS
   1 TEASPOON LEMON PEEL)
3 TABLESPOONS FRESH LIME JUICE
2 DASHES WORCESTERSHIRE SAUCE
1 TABLESPOON CURAÇAO OR OTHER ORANGE LIQUEUR
6 TABLESPOONS BITTER ORANGE MARMALADE (YOU MAY
   SUBSTITUTE STANDARD ORANGE MARMALADE)
2 TABLESPOONS GOOD-QUALITY BRANDY
1 TEASPOON GROUND RED PEPPER (CAYENNE)

Preheat the oven to 450°F. Remove any excess fat from the duck cavity and neck area. Set aside the liver, neck, and giblets for another use. Rinse duck, pat it dry, and pierce its skin all over with the tip of a knife, then rub it inside and out with salt and pepper.

Place the duck, breast side down, on a rack in a large roasting pan and roast for 1/2 hour. Reduce the heat to 275°, turn the duck over, and continue to roast for an additional 2 hours, or until the juices run clear when the thigh is pierced with a fork. (If the breast begins to get too brown before the bird is done, cover it with foil.)

Remove duck from the roasting pan and allow it to rest for 10 to 15 minutes. Meanwhile, discard excess fat from the pan juices and place the pan on the stove over medium heat. Add all the remaining ingredients and simmer for 2 to 3 minutes, stirring constantly, until the marmalade is melted and the ingredients are well blended.

Cut the duck in half, place on a platter, drizzle lightly with sauce, and pass the remaining sauce in a gravy boat.

> "No mean woman can cook well, for it calls for a light hand, a generous spirit, and a large heart."
> —PAUL GAUGUIN

LADY CAROLINE'S LAMB WITH THREE BYRONIC SAUCES

Lady Caroline Blackwood

Apricots, pomegranates, and figs are among the most voluptuous of fruits. Apricots were called "eggs of the sun" by the Persians and considered a symbol of a sensual nature by the Chinese; pomegranates are recommended as erotic aids in the Kama Sutra, among other ancient texts; and when the priests of ancient Athens announced that the figs were ripe, the news was celebrated by ritual copulation. Serves 4.

1 POUND LEAN GROUND LAMB
1 TABLESPOON MINCED FRESH GINGER
1/2 TABLESPOON MINCED GARLIC
1/2 BUNCH PARSLEY, WASHED AND FINELY CHOPPED
1 TABLESPOON TAMARI OR LIGHT SOY SAUCE
2 TABLESPOONS PLAIN NONFAT YOGURT
1 TEASPOON DRY MUSTARD
1 RED ONION, CUT INTO WEDGES
4 ZUCCHINI, CUT INTO ROUNDS ABOUT 1 1/2 INCHES THICK
POMEGRANATE SEEDS FOR GARNISH (OPTIONAL)

Preheat the broiler or light a grill. In a large bowl, combine the lamb with the ginger, garlic, parsley, tamari, yogurt, and mustard. Mix together well (your hands work best for this task) and form into 16 meatballs about 2 inches in diameter.

Thread the meatballs onto 8 small skewers along with the zucchini rounds and onion wedges. Place under the broiler or on the grill over a medium-hot fire and cook, rotating every 2 minutes, until the lamb is firm to the touch and slightly pink in the center, about 6 to 8 minutes. Serve skewered or unskewered, as you like, accompanied by apricot sauce, fig tapenade, and pomegranate sauce (*opposite*) and garnished with pomegranate seeds if desired.

An Appetite for Passion

APRICOT SAUCE

$1/2$ CUP APRICOT JAM

1 TABLESPOON DIJON MUSTARD

1 TABLESPOON TAMARI OR LIGHT SOY SAUCE

PINCH OF HORSERADISH

Whisk all ingredients together in a stainless steel bowl.

FIG TAPENADE

2 TABLESPOONS OLIVE OIL

1 SMALL WHITE ONION, DICED

1 TABLESPOON GOOD-QUALITY BRANDY

8 FRESH OR DRIED FIGS

1 TABLESPOON BROWN SUGAR

1 TABLESPOON BALSAMIC VINEGAR

$1/3$ CUP PINE NUTS, TOASTED IN A 425°F OVEN
UNTIL LIGHTLY BROWNED

In a small sauté pan, heat the olive oil until hot but not smoking, add the onion, and sauté until transparent, 5 to 7 minutes. Add the brandy and stir, making sure to scrape up any bits of browned onion adhering to the bottom of the pan. Add the figs, brown sugar, and vinegar. Allow to simmer for 5 minutes, stirring occasionally. Remove from the heat, fold in the toasted pine nuts, and serve.

POMEGRANATE SAUCE

1 POMEGRANATE

$1/2$ BUNCH CILANTRO, CLEANED AND CHOPPED

2 CLOVES GARLIC, MINCED

1 PINT PLAIN NONFAT YOGURT

$1/4$ CUP WALNUTS, TOASTED IN A 425°F OVEN
JUST UNTIL FRAGRANT

Cut the pomegranate in half and remove the seeds. Combine the cilantro, garlic, and yogurt. Fold in walnuts and pomegranate seeds before serving.

TAMARIND-SCENTED LAMB STEW

Sami Rahoumi, Houston, TX

While many formerly rare spices have become part of our everyday life, tamarind still retains a sense of mystique. Like cinnamon and ginger in medieval Europe, tamarind can still conjure up visions of mystery, of perfumed rooms and subtle, seductive glances. Here this sweet-tart spice does its conjuring in a lamb stew that also contains eggplant, another aphrodisiac from ancient Persia. Serves 6.

> 6 TAMARIND PODS (MAY SUBSTITUTE TAMARIND CONCENTRATE,
>   WHICH CAN BE FOUND IN INDIAN MARKETS)
> 4 MEDIUM EGGPLANTS, PEELED AND CUT INTO 1 1/2-INCH CUBES
> 4 TABLESPOONS VEGETABLE OIL
> 3 POUNDS BONED LEG OF LAMB, CUT INTO 1 1/2-INCH CUBES
> 1 LARGE ONION, CHOPPED FINE
> 1 1/2 TEASPOONS TURMERIC
> 1 TEASPOON SALT
> 1 TEASPOON WHITE PEPPER, OR MORE TO TASTE
> 5 LARGE TOMATOES, PURÉED IN A BLENDER OR FOOD
>   PROCESSOR
> 2 TABLESPOONS TOMATO PASTE
> 2 TABLESPOONS CHOPPED FRESH CILANTRO

Peel the tamarind pods and soak in 1 cup of warm water for 30 to 45 minutes. Mash the pulp into the water, strain, discard the solids, and reserve the liquid.

Preheat the broiler. Place the eggplant cubes on a baking sheet lightly coated with vegetable oil. Place under the broiler and brown on all sides. Remove and place on paper towels to drain. Reserve.

In a large pot over medium heat, heat the remaining vegetable oil until hot but not smoking. Add the lamb and sauté, stirring occasionally, until the cubes are well browned on all sides, about 8 to

10 minutes. Add the onion and simmer, stirring frequently, until the juices run dry, about 20 minutes. Stir constantly during the last few minutes of this process to prevent scorching. Add the turmeric, salt, and pepper and mix well.

Add the tomatoes, tomato paste, eggplant, and tamarind liquid, cover, and turn the heat to low. Simmer for 1 hour, adding a little extra water if the mixture becomes too dry. Serve over rice (preferably basmati or some other aromatic rice) and garnish with fresh cilantro.

"Cooking is like love. It should be entered into with abandon or not at all."
—HARRIET VAN HORNE

𝒫PORK TENDERLOIN WITH BLACK PLUM RELISH AND PUMPKIN SEEDS

Adapted from Complete Cuisine, Houston, TX

Pork tenderloin is an excellent dish possessing the rich flavor of pork with as little fat as a skinless breast of chicken. Here it is accompanied by a juicy black plum relish and pumpkin seeds, a tasty and traditional Mexican food. If you can't find pumpkin seeds, the dish will still be great—but you might want to consider that in much of Turkey and Eastern Europe these little seeds are considered potent aphrodisiacs. Serves 6.

> ¼ CUP RAW PUMPKIN SEEDS (PEPITAS)
> SALT
> 2 (1-POUND) PORK TENDERLOINS
> ¼ CUP EXTRA VIRGIN OLIVE OIL
> ¼ CUP FRESH LIME JUICE
> 4 CLOVES GARLIC, CRUSHED
> 1 SERRANO OR OTHER HOT CHILE PEPPER, MINCED
> 1 TEASPOON FRESHLY GROUND BLACK PEPPER
> 1 TEASPOON CHOPPED FRESH THYME

Set a heavy skillet over low heat for 2 or 3 minutes. Add the pumpkin seeds. As soon as the first one pops, begin to stir and continue to do so until all have popped and turned golden. Sprinkle lightly with salt, remove from the heat, and set aside.

Trim excess fat from the tenderloins and place them in a large shallow dish. In a small bowl, combine the oil, lime juice, garlic, chile pepper, black pepper, and thyme. Mix well and pour over the pork. Cover and refrigerate for 2 to 3 hours.

Remove the pork from the marinade and grill over a medium-hot fire, turning occasionally, for 18 to 20 minutes or until a thermometer registers an internal temperature of 155°F. Remove, allow to rest for 10 minutes, and slice into rounds about $1/4$ inch thick. Serve with black plum relish (*below*) and garnish with the pan-toasted pumpkin seeds.

BLACK PLUM RELISH

2 CUPS DICED BLACK PLUMS
1 RED BELL PEPPER, SEEDED AND DICED
$1/4$ CUP FRESH ORANGE JUICE
$1/4$ CUP SUGAR
$1/2$ TEASPOON HOT RED PEPPER FLAKES
1 TEASPOON PORT WINE

In a medium-sized bowl, combine all the ingredients and mix well. Set aside, allowing to stand at room temperature for 1 hour. Makes about 3 cups.

> "A recipe is only a theme which an intelligent cook can play each time with a variation."
> —MADAME BENOIT

BACCHANALIAN BRANDIED VENISON

The layers of flavor and the sweet alcoholic edge in a good brandy make it a natural for combining with game. In this dish, the brandy is flamed before being added to the sauce, which makes quite a dramatic moment in the kitchen. Make sure your guests are present to witness it, perhaps while sipping a glass of fine brandy themselves. Serves 4.

1 (2-POUND) VENISON TENDERLOIN
1 TABLESPOON CHOPPED FRESH ROSEMARY
3 CLOVES GARLIC, MASHED
2 TABLESPOONS HONEY
2 TABLESPOONS PLUS 1 TEASPOON DIJON MUSTARD
1 TABLESPOON OLIVE OIL
3 SHALLOTS, MINCED
2 TABLESPOONS BRANDY
1/2 CUP BEEF STOCK
2 FRESH OR DRIED FIGS, CHOPPED
2 TABLESPOONS VEGETABLE OIL
FRESH ROSEMARY SPRIGS FOR GARNISH (OPTIONAL)

Place the tenderloin in a shallow glass dish. In a food processor or blender, combine the rosemary, garlic, honey, and 2 tablespoons of mustard and process until smooth. Rub the tenderloin with this mixture, cover, and refrigerate for 2 hours.

In a small saucepan, heat the olive oil over medium heat until hot but not smoking. Add the shallots and sauté, stirring occasionally, until transparent, about 5 minutes. Add the brandy and, when heated, remove the pan from the fire and ignite the mixture with a match. The flame will quickly die out. Return the pan to the burner over medium heat, add the beef stock and the remaining teaspoon of mustard and cook, stirring, until the sauce is reduced by about half. Add the figs and cook, stirring, until the figs are just warmed through, about 2 to 3 minutes.

Preheat the oven to 400°F. In a large sauté pan, heat the vegetable oil over medium heat until hot but not smoking. Add the venison and sear well on all sides, about 3 to 4 minutes per side. Remove, place in a roasting pan, and roast for 20 to 25 minutes or until the interior is cooked through but still pink. Slice the venison into half-inch medallions, drape with the sauce, and garnish with fresh rosemary sprigs if desired.

"When from a long distant past nothing subsists after the things are broken and scattered the smell and taste of things remain."

—MARCEL PROUST

ALWAYS GAME STEW

Charlotte's Catering, New York, NY

Since Adam and Eve were first tempted by the forbidden fruit and prehistoric man stalked prey to provide nourishment for his woman, the hunt has evoked a feeling of romance and seduction. Game meats have been considered aphrodisiacal throughout history, partly because in eating them the diner partakes vicariously in the excitement of the chase, and partly because of the indefinable but visceral appeal of the taste we now call "gamy." Invite a dozen of your most adventurous friends to partake of this incredible stew. Serves 12.

STOCK

BONES FROM ALL MEATS
1 CELERY ROOT, PEELED AND CUT INTO CHUNKS
4 PARSNIPS, ROUGHLY CHOPPED
4 CARROTS, ROUGHLY CHOPPED
2 LEEKS, TRIMMED AND WELL CLEANED
3 ONIONS, PEELED AND ROUGHLY CHOPPED
1/4 CUP TOMATO PASTE

MEAT MARINADE

1 1/2 BOTTLES GOOD RED WINE
1 CUP OLIVE OIL
1/2 CUP CRUSHED JUNIPER BERRIES
4 BAY LEAVES
4 CLOVES GARLIC, PEELED
1 TABLESPOON FRESH THYME
1 TABLESPOON FRESH ROSEMARY
1 TABLESPOON DRIED MARJORAM
5 SHALLOTS, PEELED AND CHOPPED

25 DRIED MOREL MUSHROOMS
ABOUT $^1/_2$ CUP OLIVE OIL
25 WHOLE FRESH CHANTERELLE MUSHROOMS
25 WHOLE FRESH SHIITAKE MUSHROOMS
25 SMALL POTATOES, PEELED
25 SHALLOTS, PEELED
25 BABY CARROTS, PEELED
1 POUND HARICOTS VERTS, BLANCHED
25 SMALL TURNIPS, BLANCHED
1 (7-POUND) LEG OF VENISON, BONED AND CUT INTO
   CUBES (BONES RESERVED)
4 QUAIL, BONES REMOVED AND RESERVED
3 SNOW GROUSE, BONES REMOVED AND RESERVED
2 CORNISH HENS, BONES REMOVED AND RESERVED
1 HARE, BONES REMOVED AND RESERVED
SALT AND FRESHLY GROUND PEPPER TO TASTE

In a large stockpot, combine the game bones, celery root, parsnips, carrots, leeks, onions, and tomato paste. Fill the pot three-quarters full with water. Bring to a boil, reduce the heat to very low, and simmer uncovered for 48 hours. Check every few hours and add water as necessary to cover all bones and vegetables. Strain, discard the vegetables, and reserve the stock.

Combine all the marinade ingredients.

Place each type of meat in a separate bowl, and cover each with the marinade. Cover the bowls with plastic wrap and refrigerate for 24 hours.

(continued on next page)

Soak the morels in lukewarm water to cover for 30 minutes and strain. In a large sauté pan, sauté all mushrooms together in 1 tablespoon olive oil until tender, about 3 to 5 minutes.

Preheat the oven to 375°F. Place the potatoes and shallots in a large roasting pan and coat lightly with olive oil. Roast for 1 hour, turning occasionally, until golden. Salt and pepper to taste.

Strain the meats and add the marinade to the reserved stock. Boil the liquid in a large stockpot over medium heat until reduced by about one third. The resulting stock should have a strong and fairly pungent flavor.

Brown the meats separately in sauté pans over medium heat, using just enough olive oil to coat the bottom of the pans.

Put 2 quarts of stock into a large shallow pot. Add the browned venison and simmer uncovered over medium-low heat for 1 hour. Add the hare and simmer for another $1/2$ hour. Add the rest of the meats, the carrots, mushrooms, shallots, and potatoes, and let simmer for $1/2$ hour, adding more stock if necessary.

Transfer the stew to large ceramic baking dishes, place the haricots verts and turnips on top, and bake in a 350° oven for 30 to 45 minutes or until heated through. Serve in the baking dishes with huge ladles, accompanied by hearty peasant bread and rough red wine.

"The hunt was a prelude to the pursuit of love— more tender, equally carnal."

—Molière

GRILLED VENISON LOIN WITH BOURBON PEACHES

Adapted from The Thrill of the Grill *by Chris Schlesinger and John Willoughby*

Slightly gamy in taste and rife with implications of wildness, venison has a long history as an aphrodisiac. It enjoyed particular favor among medieval European paramours such as Madame du Barry, who reputedly used it to entice Louis XV to bed. This recipe features the tender loin of venison, which is best cooked quickly and served rare. In case additional stimulation is desired, it is paired with sweet-tart peaches spiked with bourbon. Serves 4 to 6.

> 1 (2¼-POUND) VENISON LOIN CUT INTO 2 PIECES CROSSWISE
> SALT AND FRESHLY GROUND BLACK PEPPER TO TASTE

Season the venison with salt and pepper and grill over a medium hot fire for 5 to 6 minutes per side until well seared. Remove and allow to rest for 5 minutes, then slice thin. If you find it too rare, grill the slices individually for a minute or so more. Serve with bourbon peaches (*below*).

BOURBON PEACHES

> 1 CUP SUGAR
> 1½ CUPS WATER
> 1 CUP CIDER VINEGAR
> 8 SMALL RIPE PEACHES, PEELED, QUARTERED, AND PITTED
> 10 WHOLE CLOVES
> ½ CUP BOURBON WHISKEY
> 4 SPRIGS FRESH MINT

Combine the sugar, water, and vinegar in a saucepan and bring to a boil. Add the peaches and cloves, simmer for 5 minutes, and remove from the heat. Allow to cool to room temperature, then pour into a quart jar. Add the bourbon and mint, cover tightly, and refrigerate for at least 1 week. Will keep for up to 6 weeks covered and refrigerated.

Every night should have its own menu.

—BALZAC

❧SIDE DISHES❧

TRUFFLED POTATO ELIXIR
Mary McFadden

So rare and delicate are truffles, and so prized their heady fragrance and musky taste, that since early times they have been associated with magic. The ancient Greeks, for example, believed that these fungi were created when thunderbolts of the gods struck the earth.

This recipe is a favorite of fashion designer Mary McFadden, whose entertaining style is as dramatic as her clothes. When serving these aphrodisiac potatoes, she places them in the center of oversized white china plates of varied patterns, all having in common a gold filigree. Serves 6.

> 2 POUNDS BAKING POTATOES, PEELED AND CUBED
> 1/2 STICK (4 TABLESPOONS) UNSALTED BUTTER
> 1/3 CUP HEAVY CREAM
> FRESHLY GROUND WHITE PEPPER TO TASTE
> 1/3 TEASPOON SALT
> 3 BLACK TRUFFLES, FINELY CHOPPED

Boil cubed potatoes until very easily pierced with a fork, about 15 minutes, then drain and mash. Whip in the butter, cream, pepper, and salt. When the potatoes are fluffy, stir in the truffles. Serve immediately.

"Beware of young women who love neither wine nor truffles nor cheese nor music."

—COLETTE

PURPLE POTATOES AND CAVIAR

Adapted from Caviar Kaspia, London, England. This is a favorite of Kenneth Lane, whose fabulous faux jewelry and wicked humor enliven many dinners.

Throughout history, people have gone to extraordinary lengths to get caviar, both for its unique taste and its alleged aphrodisiac powers. Perhaps the most extreme were the Roman aristocrats in the later days of the Empire, who had relays of slaves run live sturgeon from the Caspian Sea to Rome to ensure that their caviar was fresh. If you can't find purple potatoes for this recipe, just use red Bliss or another good baking potato. Serves 2.

> 2 PURPLE POTATOES
> UNSALTED BUTTER TO TASTE
> HEAVY CREAM TO TASTE
> SALT AND FRESHLY GROUND PEPPER TO TASTE
> CRÈME FRAÎCHE TO TASTE
> CAVIAR TO FIT YOUR BUDGET

Bake potatoes in a 425°F oven, piercing each potato deeply with a fork at least once during baking to remove steam, until a fork can easily be run all the way through them. This should take about 40 minutes to 1 hour.

Remove the potatoes from the oven, cut the tops off, and scoop out the potato. Add unsalted butter and salt and pepper to taste, then mash until every single lump is out. Mix in a bit of heavy cream to bring the potatoes to the desired consistency.

Pile the mashed potatoes back into the potato skins and place back in the oven until the potato is very hot and the skin is crispy. Garnish with crème fraîche and caviar of your choice. Best served with chilled vodka or champagne.

> **"Come quickly, I am tasting the stars!"**
> —On the discovery of Champagne

ROOT VEGETABLE MÉNAGE À TROIS

Root vegetables may not seem all that sensual when you pull them up from the ground, but their earthy flavors make wonderful, satisfying comfort food. So think of these purées as the culinary equivalent of slipping into something more comfortable. In fact, many root vegetables actually have been used as aphrodisiacs. Carrots were considered a valuable aid to seduction by Middle Eastern royalty, and the Roman emperor Nero was said to have eaten so many leeks in an attempt to improve his sexual performance that he was nicknamed "leek-eater." Each purée will serve 4 as a side dish.

ZESTY CARROT PURÉE

2 CUPS ROUGHLY CHOPPED PEELED CARROTS
2 TABLESPOONS BUTTER
1 SMALL ONION, CHOPPED
2 GRANNY SMITH APPLES, PEELED, CORED,
    AND ROUGHLY CHOPPED
2 TEASPOONS CURRY POWDER
1/2 CUP CHICKEN STOCK
1/2 CUP HEAVY CREAM
SALT AND FRESHLY GROUND PEPPER TO TASTE

Fill a large saucepan half full of water, bring to a boil, add carrots, and simmer until soft, 8 to 10 minutes. Drain and set aside. In a sauté pan over medium heat, melt the butter and add the onion, apples, and curry powder. Sauté, stirring frequently, until the onions are transparent, 5 to 7 minutes. Add the chicken stock, turn the heat to high, and boil to reduce the liquid by half. Place the apple mixture in a food processor or blender along with the cream and reserved carrots. Purée until smooth and adjust the seasoning.

"I never worry about diets. The only carrots that interest me are the number you get in a diamond."
—MAE WEST

LUSTY LEEK PURÉE

1 1/2 TABLESPOONS BUTTER
3 CLOVES GARLIC, MINCED
4 CUPS CLEANED AND CHOPPED LEEKS (WHITE PART ONLY)
1 LARGE BAKING POTATO, PEELED AND CUT INTO MEDIUM DICE
3 TABLESPOONS GRATED PARMESAN CHEESE
2 TABLESPOONS HEAVY CREAM
2 TABLESPOONS NONFAT SOUR CREAM
SALT AND FRESHLY GROUND PEPPER TO TASTE

In a large sauté pan over medium heat, melt the butter and sauté the garlic and leeks, stirring frequently, until the leeks are soft, about 10 to 12 minutes. Fill a large saucepan half full of water, bring to a boil, and simmer the potato until soft, approximately 10 minutes. Drain. Combine all the ingredients in a blender, purée until smooth, and adjust the seasoning.

EARTHY BEET PURÉE

2 1/2 POUNDS BEETS, UNPEELED
1 1/2 TABLESPOONS PREPARED HORSERADISH
2 TEASPOONS BALSAMIC VINEGAR
3 TABLESPOONS NONFAT YOGURT
SALT AND FRESHLY GROUND PEPPER TO TASTE

Bring a large pot of water to a boil, add the beets, and cook until the beets are easily pierced by a fork, about 40 minutes. Slip off the skins. Place the beets in a food processor or blender with all the other ingredients, purée until smooth, and adjust the seasoning.

SULTRY GRILLED ASPARAGUS

Nicholas Culpepper, a well-known herbalist of the seventeenth century, declared that "Asparagus stirreth up bodily lust in both men and women." To help it accomplish this task, we coat it with Asian-flavored glaze, put it over the flames for a few minutes so it takes on a smoky flavor, then serve it with juicy orange sections and tangy onions. Serves 4.

> 1 1/2 POUNDS FRESH ASPARAGUS
> 1/4 CUP SOY SAUCE
> 2 TABLESPOONS FRESH ORANGE JUICE
> 2 TEASPOONS MINCED GARLIC
> 1 TEASPOON MINCED FRESH CHILE PEPPER (OPTIONAL)
> SALT AND FRESHLY GROUND BLACK PEPPER TO TASTE
> 1/4 RED ONION, SLICED VERY THIN
> 1 ORANGE, PEELED, SEEDED, SECTIONED, AND SECTIONS HALVED

Rinse the asparagus and snap off the tough ends.

In a small bowl, combine the soy sauce, orange juice, garlic, and chile pepper if desired. Mix very well.

Brush the soy-orange mixture over the asparagus stalks, sprinkle them liberally with salt and pepper, and grill over a medium-hot fire, rolling occasionally to ensure even cooking, for about 8 or 10 minutes, or until the stalks are just lightly browned and cooked through. If there is any soy mixture left over, brush it over the asparagus during the last 30 seconds of cooking.

Arrange the asparagus on a platter, garnish with onion slices and orange sections, and serve.

> **"You needn't tell me that a man who doesn't love oysters
> and asparagus and good wines has got a soul."**
>
> —SAKI

LPEAS FROM A PERFUMED GARDEN

Many of the ancient recipes for aphrodisiacal potions turn out to be more like medicine than food. In the Persian erotic classic *The Perfumed Garden*, however, the author suggests making a love potion by cooking green peas with onions and spices, including the wonderfully aromatic cardamom. Serves 2 to 3 as a side dish.

2 TEASPOONS EXTRA VIRGIN OLIVE OIL

$1/2$ RED ONION, SLICED VERY THIN

1 CUP SHELLED FRESH GREEN PEAS (OR FROZEN PEAS, BROKEN UP)

$1/2$ CUP WATER

$1/4$ TEASPOON GROUND CINNAMON

1 TEASPOON MINCED FRESH GINGER

$1/4$ TEASPOON GROUND CARDAMOM

SALT TO TASTE

2 OR 3 WHOLE FRESH MINT LEAVES

In a sauté pan, heat the olive oil over medium heat until hot but not smoking. Add the onion and sauté until just tender, about 4 minutes. Add the peas, water, cinnamon, ginger, and cardamom, and season lightly with salt. Stir to combine and bring to a boil. Reduce the heat to low and simmer until the peas are just cooked through and tender, about 8 to 10 minutes (3 to 4 minutes if frozen). During the last minute or so, stir in the mint leaves. Adjust seasoning and serve.

"Green peas, boiled carefully with onions, and powdered with cinnamon, ginger, and cardamoms well pounded, create for the consumer considerable amorous passion and strength for love."
—CHEIKH NEFZAONTI, *The Perfumed Garden*

I can resist everything except temptation.

—OSCAR WILDE

⊗DESSERTS⊗

CHOCOLATE GOURMET LA VEGA

Carolina Herrera

Carolina Herrera, an international beauty and fashion designer, has served this chocolate extravaganza to such luminaries as Arthur Rubinstein, the great pianist; HRH Prince Charles, Prince of Wales; and Christian Dior. "Chocolate Gourmet la Vega" was created in Venezuela at the turn of the twentieth century by Rafael Ortega, the chef of Mrs. Herrera's great-grandmother-in-law. Serves 4 to 6.

12 OUNCES DARK SEMISWEET CHOCOLATE
3/4 CUP (1 1/2 STICKS) UNSALTED BUTTER, AT ROOM
    TEMPERATURE
1 1/2 CUPS SUGAR
6 LARGE EGGS, SEPARATED
1 TABLESPOON FLOUR

Preheat the oven to 350°F.

Melt the chocolate in a double boiler on top of the stove. Remove from the heat, add the softened butter, and stir until the butter is melted and well combined with the chocolate. Add the sugar and stir well. Add the egg yolks one at a time, stirring well after each addition.

Beat the egg whites until they form soft peaks, sprinkling in 1 tablespoon of flour toward the end of the beating.

Fold the egg whites into the chocolate mixture, pour into an 8 x 10-inch mold or ramekin, and bake until just set, about 45 minutes. Serve with crème anglaise if desired.

"Pleasure's a sin and sometimes sin's a pleasure."
—LORD BYRON

ICE CREAM WITH CRUSHED PRALINES

At harvest festivals in ancient Rome, young maidens traditionally passed out bowls of nuts to the men as tokens of fertility. Soon it became the custom to give nuts to newlyweds, and eventually the groom's friends threw nuts into the bedroom of the newlyweds on their wedding night. This is a quick and easy dessert when scooped on top of ice cream. Makes 4 to 6 servings.

> 1 CUP SUGAR
> PINCH OF CREAM OF TARTAR
> 1/4 CUP WATER
> 1 CUP BLANCHED ALMONDS
> ICE CREAM

In a heavy skillet, dissolve the sugar and cream of tartar in the water over moderate heat. Bring to a boil, stirring constantly. Bring syrup to a boil, and continue stirring until the syrup becomes caramel colored. Add the almonds and swirl the skillet until all the nuts are coated with the caramel.

Pour the mixture onto a piece of buttered foil and allow to cool completely. Transfer to a cutting board, chop coarsely, and crush in batches in a food processor or blender. Serve on top of ice cream. Pralines will keep for 3 weeks in an airtight container.

WARM CHOCOLATE SOUFFLÉ

Kenya Hemingway Safari

A light, airy soufflé always seems like a culinary miracle. In the hands of sorcerers, it was believed, this dark, weirdly irresistible substance could inspire wild behavior of all varieties. This warm soufflé is a favorite at Abercrombie and Kent's romantic African safari. Serves 8 to 10.

3/4 CUP UNSWEETENED COCOA POWDER

3/4 PLUS 1/4 CUP SUGAR

1/2 CUP UNSIFTED ALL-PURPOSE FLOUR

1/8 TEASPOON SALT

2 CUPS MILK

6 EGG YOLKS, WELL BEATEN

2 TABLESPOONS UNSALTED BUTTER

1 TEASPOON VANILLA EXTRACT

8 EGG WHITES, AT ROOM TEMPERATURE

1/4 TEASPOON CREAM OF TARTAR

SWEETENED WHIPPED CREAM

Lightly butter a 2 1/2-quart soufflé dish and sprinkle with sugar. Measure a length of heavy-duty aluminum foil to fit around the dish; fold in thirds lengthwise. Lightly oil one side of the foil and tape it securely to the outside of the dish with the oiled side facing in; be sure the top of this collar extends at least 2 inches above the rim of the dish and the bottom is at least 1 1/2 inches from the bottom of the dish. Set aside.

Combine the cocoa, 3/4 cup sugar, flour, and salt in a medium saucepan, then gradually stir in the milk. Cook over medium heat, stirring constantly with a wire whisk, until the mixture boils. Immediately remove from the heat. Gradually stir a small amount of the chocolate mixture into the egg yolks, blending well. Return the egg mixture to the chocolate mixture in the saucepan. Add the butter and vanilla and stir until well combined. Set aside to cool to lukewarm. Meanwhile, preheat the oven to 350°F.

Beat the egg whites with the cream of tartar in a large bowl until soft peaks form. Add the 1/4 cup sugar, 2 tablespoons at a time, beating until stiff peaks form. Gently fold one third of the chocolate mixture into the egg whites, then fold in the remaining chocolate mixture one half at a time, just until combined.

Carefully pour the mixture, without stirring, into the prepared dish and smooth the top with a spatula. Place the dish in a larger pan and set on the bottom rack of the oven. Pour hot water into the outer pan to a depth of 1 inch. Bake for 1 hour and 10 minutes, or until the soufflé is puffy and has risen several inches above the rim of the dish. Carefully remove the foil and serve immediately accompanied by whipped cream.

**"Making love without love
is like trying to make a soufflé without eggs."**
—Simone Beck

CHOCOLATE PYRAMIDS
Jimmy Schmidt, Rattlesnake Club, Detroit, MI

In certain monasteries in the seventeenth century, chocolate was forbidden because of its supposed powers of sexual arousal. While that may be an exaggeration, the sinful richness of this dark, dense chocolate cake is quite likely to cause you to explore further indulgences of the senses. Serves 4.

22 OUNCES BITTERSWEET CHOCOLATE

2 TABLESPOONS UNSALTED BUTTER PLUS ADDITIONAL BUTTER
    FOR SECURING MOLDS

1 1/2 CUPS HEAVY CREAM

1/2 CUP UNSWEETENED COCOA POWDER

1 CUP PEACH PURÉE

1/2 CUP RASPBERRY PURÉE

1/2 PINT FRESH RASPBERRIES

16 FRESH MINT LEAVES

Prepare the molds: Choose 4 pyramids or other molds, each about 8 ounces in volume. Line all of the interior surfaces of the molds with parchment paper and secure in place with a dab of butter between the paper and the mold. Refrigerate the molds.

Place 12 ounces of the chocolate in the upper half of a double boiler and heat over medium heat, stirring constantly, until almost completely melted. Remove from the heat and stir until the chocolate has completely melted to form a thick, smooth coating just warm to the touch. Using a pastry brush, paint the insides of the molds until solidly covered, returning each mold to the refrigerator as it is done. When all the molds have been covered, repeat the process to form a second thin chocolate coat, then refrigerate molds. As the melted chocolate thickens, place it over warm water until it reaches the desired consistency.

Prepare the mousse: In the top of a double boiler, combine the remaining 10 ounces of chocolate and the 2 tablespoons of butter. Heat over medium heat, stirring constantly, until completely melted and very warm, about 10 minutes. In another bowl, whip the cream until just foamy, not thickened like whipped cream. Remove the chocolate from the heat, add one third of the cream to the chocolate, and fold to combine. Repeat with another one third of the cream. Finally add the remaining cream and fold until smooth and homogenous but not thickened. Ladle the mousse into the prepared molds. Refrigerate until firm, at least 12 hours.

Unmold the pyramids onto a cookie sheet. Place the cocoa in a fine sieve and sift over the molds to evenly coat the exteriors. Transfer the pyramids to the center of 4 serving plates. Spoon the peach purée around the pyramids, fill a squirt bottle with raspberry purée, and squirt over the peach purée on the plate in a wild zigzag pattern. Garnish with raspberries and mint leaves and serve.

"Love and gluttony justify everything."
—Oscar Wilde

CHOCOLATE FONDUE
WITH EXOTIC FRUITS

Jacques Torres, Le Cirque, New York, NY

One of Cortés's men, Bernal Díaz del Castillo, writes that servants used to bring the Aztec ruler Montezuma cups made of pure gold containing a bitter chocolate drink to increase his vigor before visiting his wives. Today, chocolate's aphrodisiac qualities persist in the custom of giving boxes of chocolates as Valentine's Day gifts. Here the royal aphrodisiac is served with tropical fruits for dipping. Serves 4.

FRUIT AS DESIRED FOR DIPPING: CARAMBOLAS, MANGOES,
STRAWBERRIES, BLOOD ORANGES, RASPBERRIES, ETC.
10½ OUNCES BITTERSWEET CHOCOLATE
1½ CUPS HEAVY CREAM
2 TABLESPOONS CHARTREUSE VERTE OR OTHER LIQUEUR

Peel, core, or seed the fruit as necessary to prepare for eating out of hand.

Chop the chocolate into small pieces and set aside.

In a heavy-bottomed saucepan, bring 1 cup of the heavy cream to a boil over medium heat, stirring constantly to avoid scalding. Add the chocolate and blend together using a hand blender or whisk until very smooth. Blend in the Chartreuse, pour the fondue into a ramekin set in the center of a platter, and arrange the fruits around the ramekin for dipping. Serve at once.

> **"Sharing food with another human being is an intimate act
> that should not be indulged in lightly."**
> —M.F.K. FISHER, *An Alphabet for Gourmets*, "A is for Dining Alone"

BLOOD ORANGE SOUP
Chanterelle, New York, NY

The brilliant red flesh of blood oranges lends an air of exotic rarity to this sweet-tart fruit. For this light and refreshing dessert, blood orange juice is sweetened, spiked with liqueur, and combined with berries and seasonal fruits. If you are short on time, you can omit the sorbet from this soup entirely, or use store-bought orange or raspberry sorbet. In that case, cut the amount of the first four ingredients by half. Serves 4.

12 BLOOD ORANGES, JUICED
1 CUP SUGAR
2 TABLESPOONS GRAND MARNIER OR OTHER ORANGE LIQUEUR
2 TABLESPOONS FRESH LEMON JUICE
1/4 PINT RASPBERRIES
1/4 PINT STRAWBERRIES, STEMMED AND QUARTERED
1/2 GRAPEFRUIT, PEELED AND SECTIONED
1/2 CANTALOUPE OR OTHER SMALL MELON, SCOOPED
   INTO BALLS

Strain the orange juice into a large bowl. Add the sugar, Grand Marnier, and lemon juice and mix well. Divide this mixture in half. Refrigerate one half of the mixture and freeze the remaining half in an ice cream freezer, following the directions for sorbet.

To serve the soup, put the juice into bowls, divide the berries and seasonal fruit among the bowls, and garnish with a scoop of sorbet.

"Every fruit has its secret."
—D. H. LAWRENCE

CREAMY FRESH COCONUT DESSERT

Adapted from Authentic Mexican *by Rick and Deann Bayless*

Rick Bayless describes this Mexican dessert as a "macaroon in pudding form," and it is every bit as oozingly delicious as that sounds. Besides, there is something about the process of starting with what is basically a large nut and ending up with a yielding, lightly browned, quivering dessert, rich with sherry and egg yolks and almonds, that makes you feel like a kind of culinary wonderworker. Your guests are likely to feel the same way. Serves 6 to 8.

> 1 MEDIUM-SIZED (ABOUT $1^3/4$ POUNDS) FRESH COCONUT
> 1 CUP SUGAR
> $1^1/2$ TABLESPOONS GOOD QUALITY SHERRY
> 6 LARGE EGG YOLKS
> 3 TABLESPOONS MILK
> $1/2$ CUP SLICED ALMONDS, TOASTED IN A 325°F OVEN FOR
>   ABOUT 10 MINUTES UNTIL LIGHTLY BROWNED
> $1/2$ TABLESPOON UNSALTED BUTTER, CUT INTO SMALL BITS

Twist a corkscrew or drive a screwdriver into 2 of the 3 holes in the coconut, drain out the liquid, strain, and set aside. Place the coconut in a preheated 325°F oven for 15 minutes to loosen the shell. Remove, crack into large pieces with a hammer, and pry the meat from the shell. Trim the dark skin from the coconut using a vegetable peeler, then grate the meat.

Measure the coconut liquid and add enough water to bring the total volume to 1 cup. Place the grated coconut in a medium-sized heavy saucepan, stir in the liquid and the sugar and cook over medium heat, stirring frequently, until the coconut becomes transparent and the liquid is reduced to a glaze, about 20 to 30 minutes. Stir in the sherry and cook an additional 3 minutes, then remove from the heat.

Beat the egg yolks with the milk, stir in several tablespoons of the hot coconut, then carefully stir the warm yolk mixture into the remaining coconut. Return to medium-low heat and cook, stirring constantly, until slightly thickened, about 5 minutes. Scrape into an ovenproof serving dish.

Shortly before serving, preheat the broiler. Dot the mixture with butter and place under the broiler for only a minute or so, just until it is brown, watching carefully so that it does not burn. Remove from the broiler, scatter the toasted almonds over the top, and serve.

"Bring on the dessert. . . . I think I am about to die."
—PIERETTE, Sister of Brillat-Savarin, shortly before her 100th birthday

ROSE PETAL FLAN

Rubicon, San Francisco, CA

No flower has been more widely used as an aphrodisiac than the rose. Ancient Romans slipped the fragrant petals into their love potions and even declared an official holiday, Rosalia, in honor of this tantalizing flower. Persians made rose water a staple of their cooking, and Cleopatra was said to have lined the floor of her boudoir with rose petals so that, as her lovers approached, the air would fill with the delicate, stirring scent of roses. Serves 4 to 6.

> 4 EGG YOLKS
> 1/4 CUP SUGAR
> 2 CUPS HEAVY CREAM
> 1/2 VANILLA BEAN (YOU MAY SUBSTITUTE 1/2 TEASPOON
>   VANILLA EXTRACT)
> 1 DROP ROSE FLOWER WATER
> 1 1/2 TEASPOONS GRAND MARNIER OR OTHER
>   ORANGE-FLAVORED LIQUEUR
> PETALS FROM 2 ROSES
> FRESH RASPBERRIES OR STRAWBERRIES FOR GARNISH

Preheat the oven to 250°F.

Whisk the yolks together with the sugar in a medium-sized bowl.

Combine the cream and vanilla bean in a saucepan and place over medium heat. As soon as bubbles form around the edge of the pan, remove from the heat.

Pour half the scalded cream into the egg mixture, whisking to combine. Pour the mixture of yolks and cream back into the saucepan and cook over medium heat, stirring constantly, until the mixture coats the back of a wooden spoon.

Strain the cream mixture into a stainless steel bowl and stir in the rose water and Grand Marnier. Pour the mixture into 4 to 6 ramekins or custard cups. Set the ramekins in a large roasting pan and fill the pan with enough hot water to come about three quarters of the way up the ramekins. Bake for 40 to 50 minutes, until set. Chill for at least 2 hours. Garnish each ramekin with rose petals and fresh berries.

**"A woman is a well served table
that one sees with different eyes after the meal."**

—BALZAC

BANANA CRÈME BRÛLÉE

Adapted from Bouley, New York, NY

Serves 4.

> 1 CUP MILK
> 1 CUP HEAVY CREAM
> 2 VANILLA BEANS
> 4 RIPE BANANAS, MASHED
> 4 EGG YOLKS
> 1 CUP GRANULATED SUGAR
> ABOUT 3 TABLESPOONS BROWN SUGAR

Preheat the oven to 300°F. In a small saucepot, combine the milk and cream. Use a paring knife to split the vanilla beans and scrape out the seeds. Add the vanilla seeds to the milk and cream and bring the mixture just to a boil over medium heat, stirring constantly. Remove from the heat.

In a large bowl, combine the mashed bananas, egg yolks, and granulated sugar, and whisk until well combined. Slowly add the scalded milk mixture to the banana mixture, whisking constantly and watching to be sure the eggs do not cook.

Strain the mixture through a sieve, discard the solids, and pour the liquid into 4 ramekins or custard cups. Place in a shallow baking pan. Fill the pan with hot water three quarters of the way up the sides of the ramekins and bake for 40 minutes. The custard should still be soft. Remove from the water bath, allow to cool, and refrigerate if not serving at once.

Just before serving, sprinkle a thin, even layer of brown sugar over the top of each custard and set the ramekins in a shallow bowl of crushed ice. Place under a preheated broiler just until the sugar melts and caramelizes, about 2 minutes. Watch carefully to be sure the sugar does not burn. Remove from the ice and serve.

An Appetite for Passion

FLAMING CARAMEL BANANAS

Adapted from Martha Stewart Living

Something about flames ignites passion. The steady flame of
candlelight, the flickering flames of a wood fire, the blue flame that
licks over food as alcohol burns off—all stir amorous feelings. For a
dramatic ending to a sensual dinner, flame these bananas tableside,
then spoon over slightly softened ice cream. Serves 6.

> 1 CUP ALL-PURPOSE FLOUR
> 6 FIRM, RIPE BANANAS, PEELED, HALVED LENGTHWISE,
>   AND CUT INTO 2-INCH PIECES
> 1/3 CUP (5 1/3 TABLESPOONS) UNSALTED BUTTER
> 1/2 CUP FIRMLY PACKED BROWN SUGAR
> 1/2 CUP DARK RUM
> VANILLA ICE CREAM

Preheat the broiler. Place the flour in a large shallow dish and roll the
bananas in the flour until lightly coated.

In a large, heavy flameproof skillet, melt the butter over medium
heat. Add the bananas and sauté for 1 minute, stirring. Sprinkle the
sugar over the bananas and place the skillet under the broiler until
the sugar browns and hardens, watching carefully to be sure it does
not burn.

Remove the skillet from the broiler and pour the rum over the
bananas. Ignite with a match and cook over low heat until the
flames subside. Simmer, stirring frequently, until the sauce thickens,
about 3 to 5 minutes. Spoon the sauce over vanilla ice cream and
serve immediately.

DOUBLE MOCHA BROWNIES

Adapted from A Craving for Something Sweet *by Jack Bishop*

Coffee and chocolate are one of the most popular of culinary marriages. Both partners in this taste duo are considered potent aphrodisiacs, perhaps because both contain the stimulant caffeine. Here this happy flavor relationship is enshrined in easy, tasty brownies. Makes 12 small or 6 large brownies.

> 8 TABLESPOONS (1 STICK) UNSALTED BUTTER
> 2 (1-OUNCE) SQUARES UNSWEETENED CHOCOLATE
> 3 TABLESPOONS KAHLÚA OR OTHER COFFEE LIQUEUR
> 1 TABLESPOON INSTANT COFFEE GRANULES
> 2/3 CUP FLOUR
> 1/2 TEASPOON BAKING POWDER
> 1/4 TEASPOON SALT
> 1 CUP SUGAR
> 2 LARGE EGGS
> 1 TEASPOON VANILLA EXTRACT

Preheat the oven to 350°F. Grease an 8-inch square baking pan.

Place the butter, chocolate, Kahlúa, and instant coffee in a medium-size saucepan over low heat. Stir occasionally until the butter and chocolate have melted. (Or microwave ingredients on Medium power until melted, about 1 1/2 minutes, and stir until smooth.) Set the mixture aside to cool briefly.

In a small bowl, whisk together the flour, baking powder, and salt. Set aside.

Stir the sugar into the cooled chocolate mixture, then beat in the eggs and vanilla until the mixture is smooth. Fold in the dry ingredients. Scrape this batter into the prepared pan.

Bake until a toothpick inserted halfway between the edge and the center of the pan comes out clean, about 22 to 25 minutes. Transfer the pan to a rack and cut brownies when cool.

"I have taken more out of alcohol than alcohol has taken out of me."
—WINSTON CHURCHILL

WARM RIPE FIGS ON A BED OF ROSES WITH WILDFLOWER HONEY

Jeff Salaway

Honey—thick and slow and sweet and tasting of delicate flowers—has been used by virtually every civilization to arouse desire. Sensuous in texture and shape, figs have also been used as a food of love since pre-Biblical days. Mix these two in an elegant creation with a handful of soft and fragrant rose petals, and you have a dish that drips with romance. Serves 6.

FOR THE ROSE-PETAL CRÊPES

> 5 EGGS
> 1/2 TEASPOON SALT
> 1 CUP FLOUR
> 1 1/2 CUPS MILK
> 1/4 CUP UNSALTED BUTTER, MELTED
> GRATED ZEST OF 2 ORANGES
> PETALS FROM 2 PINK ROSES, CHOPPED FINE
> ABOUT 3 TABLESPOONS MELTED BUTTER FOR FRYING

> 12 RIPE BLACK MISSION FIGS
> 3 TABLESPOONS BUTTER
> 3/4 CUP WILDFLOWER HONEY
> 3 TABLESPOONS GOOD QUALITY BRANDY

Make the crêpes: Combine the eggs, salt, flour, and milk in a bowl and stir until smooth. Stir in the 1/4 cup melted butter, then fold in the orange zest and rose petals. Cover and refrigerate for one hour. Heat a crêpe pan or small sauté pan over medium heat. Add 2 tablespoons of melted butter, swirl it around to coat the pan well, and pour the excess back. Quickly add a small ladleful of batter, turning and shaking the pan so the base is completely coated. Fry quickly over medium high heat until the crêpe is set on top and browned beneath. Loosen with a spatula, turn quickly using both hands, and cook until the other side is brown. Repeat until all batter has been used. Set crêpes aside. Makes about 14 to 16 crêpes.

Preheat oven to 425°F. Wash the figs and cut them lengthwise into quarters, but do not cut quite all the way through the base. Place 3 fingers under the base of the figs and push the meat up through. Place the figs on an ovenproof tray and dot each with a bit of butter, using about 1 tablespoon butter total. Bake until hot and soft, about 8 minutes. Remove and set aside.

Meanwhile, combine the brandy, honey, and remaining butter in a saucepan and heat over low heat until butter is melted. Keep warm.

Take the prepared crêpes and julienne them as finely as possible, to the texture of angel hair. Divide the julienned crêpes among 6 plates, forming them into delicate nests. Place 2 figs at the center of each nest, drizzle honey mixture over all, and place under the broiler for 1 minute to warm and slightly caramelize, being careful not to let the tops burn.

> **"He who feels that he is weak for love should drink before starting out a glassful of very thick honey and eat twenty almonds and one hundred grains of the pine tree."**
> —CHEIKH NEFZAONTI, *The Perfumed Garden*

The difficulty lies not in the use of a bad thing but in the abuse of a very good thing.

—ABRAHAM LINCOLN

❧DRINKS❧

TROPICAL MIMOSA

For ceremonial occasions and wild nights, there's nothing like Champagne. This drink has it all: alcohol to release inhibitions, bursting bubbles to tickle your nose, and a legendary air of festivity and luxurious extravagance. Madame de Pompadour said that it was the only wine a woman could drink without looking ugly, and here's the proof—it was the only alcohol that Marilyn Monroe would drink.

Champagne has become a popular brunch beverage when combined with orange juice in a mimosa. After all, why restrict romance to the evening hours? Here we add a warm-weather twist by substituting tropical fruit nectar for the orange juice. You can measure the ingredients if you wish, but pouring them out by eye in a ratio of about one part juice to three parts Champagne is more in line with the spirit of the drink. Makes 1 drink.

2 OUNCES MANGO, GUAVA, PASSION FRUIT, OR PEACH NECTAR
6 OUNCES CHAMPAGNE OR OTHER SPARKLING WINE
VERY THIN PIECE OF LEMON ZEST AT LEAST 1 INCH LONG

Pour the fruit nectar into a Champagne flute and fill with Champagne. Wrap lemon zest around a toothpick to form into a spiral, then remove from the toothpick and float in the drink as a garnish.

> **"There comes a time in every woman's life when the only thing that helps is a glass of Champagne."**
> —BETTE DAVIS, *Old Acquaintance*

An Appetite for Passion

AMOROUS MARGARITA

In every country of the world, there is a colorless local liquor distilled from whatever fruit or vegetable is most abundant. Russians transform potatoes into vodka, Brazilians make sugar cane into the brandy-like cachaca, and in Mexico the heart of the agave cactus is transformed into mescal, of which tequila is one local variety. These potions are sometimes a little rough on the tongue, but a few shots at the local watering hole and you'll be ready for romance, because there's nothing more likely to stir amorous feeling than liquor in moderation.

Golden tequila is particularly good in this version of the classic tart cocktail. To go further down the gold path, add a splash of brandy for a golden margarita. Makes 1 drink.

> 2 OUNCES GOOD-QUALITY TEQUILA
> 1 OUNCE COINTREAU
> 2 TABLESPOONS FRESH LIME JUICE
> 1 TEASPOON SUGAR
> 1/2 DOZEN ICE CUBES
> KOSHER SALT

In a shaker, combine all ingredients except the salt. Stir well to dissolve the sugar.

Meanwhile, rub a squeezed lime half along the rim of the serving glass, and dip the rim in the kosher salt to lightly coat. Strain the drink into the glass.

**"Two things a man cannot hide:
that he is drunk, and that he is in love."**

—ANTIPHANES

SUNNY AFTERNOON SANGRÍA

Wine is a great romance-enhancer, but on hot afternoons it may not hit the spot. On those occasions, try mixing it up with fruit juices in a classic sangría, ancestor of the modern wine cooler. Since sangría has a relatively low alcohol content, sipping several glasses while sitting in the sun is likely to put you in the proper mood.

This version of sangría is Spanish-influenced. In Mexico, sangría tends to be more of a lime-wine mixture, with the occasional splash of tequila—which is actually not a bad idea even in this incarnation. Serves 4.

^{1}/2 CUP SUPERFINE SUGAR
^{1}/2 CUP FRESH LIME JUICE
^{1}/2 CUP FRESH ORANGE JUICE
1 BOTTLE RED TABLE WINE (ZINFANDEL IS A GOOD CHOICE)
1 ORANGE, HALVED AND SLICED THIN
1 LEMON, HALVED AND SLICED VERY THIN
1 LIME, HALVED AND SLICED VERY THIN

Combine the sugar, lime juice, and orange juice and stir very well to dissolve the sugar. Add the red wine, pour into a large pitcher with ice cubes, and stir in the fruit.

If you're having a group over, double the recipe and serve it in a punch bowl with the fruit floating on top.

> **"In water one sees one's own face, but in wine one beholds the heart of another."**
> —FRENCH PROVERB

BLACK VELVET

Leixlip Castle, County Kildare, Ireland

Desmond Guinness, scion of the legendary Irish brewing family, is said to have charmed many a lass with this heady combination of Champagne and the family's stout. You can measure the two beverages out in ounces if you want, but it's more fun to just splash equal amounts of each into a glass, give it a stir, and serve it up. Serves 1.

> 4 OUNCES GUINNESS STOUT
> 4 OUNCES GOOD-QUALITY CHAMPAGNE

Pour into a Champagne glass, stir, and serve. That's all there is to it.

"My only regret in life is that I did not drink more Champagne."
—JOHN MAYNARD KEYNES

MEXICAN SPICED COFFEE

> 2 CUPS VERY STRONG COFFEE
> 1 STICK CINNAMON (YOU MAY SUBSTITUTE 1 TEASPOON GROUND CINNAMON)
> 4 WHOLE CLOVES
> 1/4 CUP PACKED DARK BROWN SUGAR
> 1/4 TO 1/2 CUP KAHLÚA
> FRESHLY WHIPPED CREAM (OPTIONAL)

In a small saucepan, stir the cinnamon, cloves, sugar, and Kahlúa into the coffee. Heat over medium heat, stirring occasionally, until the sugar has completely dissolved. Serve topped with the whipped cream.

"Coffee should be black as Hell, strong as death, and sweet as love."
—TURKISH PROVERB

SELECTED BIBLIOGRAPHY

Ackerman, Diane. *A Natural History of the Senses.*
New York: Random House, 1990.

Ashe, Penelope. *The Naked Chef.* New York: Ashely Books, 1971.

Bolitho, Hector. *The Glorious Oyster.* New York: Horizon Press, 1960.

Brillat-Savarin. *The Physiology of Taste* (translated by M. F. K. Fisher).
New York: Alfred A. Knopf, 1971.

Cheikh Nefzaonti. *The Perfumed Garden* (translated by Richard Burton).
Golden Hind Press, 1933.

Elkort, Martin. *The Secret Life of Food.*
Los Angeles: Jeremy P. Tarcher, 1991.

Hendrickson, Robert. *Foods for Love.* New York: Stein, 1971.

Herbst, Sharon Tyler. *A Food Lover's Companion.* New York: Barron's, 1990.

Pillar, Phillipa. *Consuming Passion.* Boston: Little, Brown & Co., 1970.

Revel, Jean-Francois. *Culture and Cuisine.*
New York: Doubleday & Company, 1982.

Root, Waverley. *Food.* New York: Simon & Schuster, 1980.

Schivelbusch, Wolfgang. *Tastes of Paradise.* New York: Pantheon, 1992.

Toussaint-Samat, Maguelonne. *A History of Food.*
Cambridge: Blackwell Publishers, 1992.

Walker, Barbara G. *A Woman's Dictionary of Symbols and Sacred Objects.*
San Francisco: HarperSanFrancisco, 1988.

ACKNOWLEDGMENTS

Most importantly we thank Laura Esquivel and Alfonso Arau for their extraordinary vision and talent, and Harvey and Bob Weinstein of Miramax Films for their support.

Special thanks to Donna Daniels, Scott Greenstein, and Francesca Gonshaw of Miramax Books, whose inspiration and commitment made this book possible.

We also thank Ann Swain for her tireless efforts adapting and creating most of the recipes.

The editors would also like to thank the following for their contributions:

Michael Aaron, Sherry Lehman; Christian Albin, The Four Seasons, New York; Rick Bayless, Frontera Grill and Topolobampo; Jack Bishop, *A Craving for Something Sweet;* Mark Bittman; David Bouley, Bouley, New York; Christa Branch, Abercrombie and Kent; Kimberley Charles, Taittinger Champagne; Complete Cuisine, Houston; Eastern Orient Express; Susan Feniger and Mary Sue Milliken, Border Grill, Santa Monica; Thomas Ferlesh; Justin Fry, Galatoires, New Orleans; Desmond Guinness; Barbara Haber, Schlesinger Library, Radcliffe College, Cambridge; David Hale and Jeff Tucci, Auberge du Soleil, Napa Valley; Carolina Herrera; Josephine Howard, Rosa Mexicana, New York; Traci des Jardins and Elizabeth Falkner, Rubicon, San Francisco; Annabel Jobe, Caviar Kaspia, London; Steve Johnson; Nan Kempner; Kenya Hemingway Safari; Kenneth Lane; Marguerite Littman; *Martha Stewart Living;* Naomi Martinez, Zarela, New York; Mary McFadden; Mikael Moller, Charlotte's, New York; Sami Rahoumi, Houston; Kevin Rathbun; Anne Rosenzweig, Arcadia, New York; Jeff Salaway, Nick & Toni's, East Hampton; Coke Ann Saunders, Maidstone Inn, East Hampton; Chris Schlesinger, Blue Room, Cambridge; Jimmy Schmidt, Rattlesnake Club, Detroit; James Sherwin, The Carlyle, New York; Bruce Sobol, Caviarteria, New York; Claude Taittinger, Taittinger Champagne; Jacques Torres, Le Cirque, New York; Marla Trump; David Waltuck, Chanterelle, New York; Sara Widness; Wolfgang Winter, Relais and Chateau; Peter Zimmer, Inn of the Anasazi, Santa Fe.

INDEX